APR 2017

FIZZOPOLIS

Snoodles!

PATRICK CARMAN

Illustrated by
BRIAN SHEESLEY

 KATHERINE TEGEN BOOKS
An Imprint of HarperCollins Publishers

HarperCollins Publishers
Since 1817

Katherine Tegen Books is an imprint of
HarperCollins Publishers.

Fizzopolis: Snoodles!

For information address HarperCollins Children's Books, a division of HarperCollins Publishers, 195 Broadway, New York, NY 10007.
www.harpercollinschildrens.com

Library of Congress Control Number: 2016940298
ISBN 978-0-06-239394-4

Typography by Joel Tippie
17 18 19 20 21 CG/LSCH 10 9 8 7 6 5 4 3 2 1
❖
First Edition

This one is for Benjamin Rosenthal.
A ten-burp salute to our editor extraordinaire!
—P.C.

For Mom and Dad,
the BEST teachers ever
who encouraged me to dream…
and to have a backup plan.
—B.S.

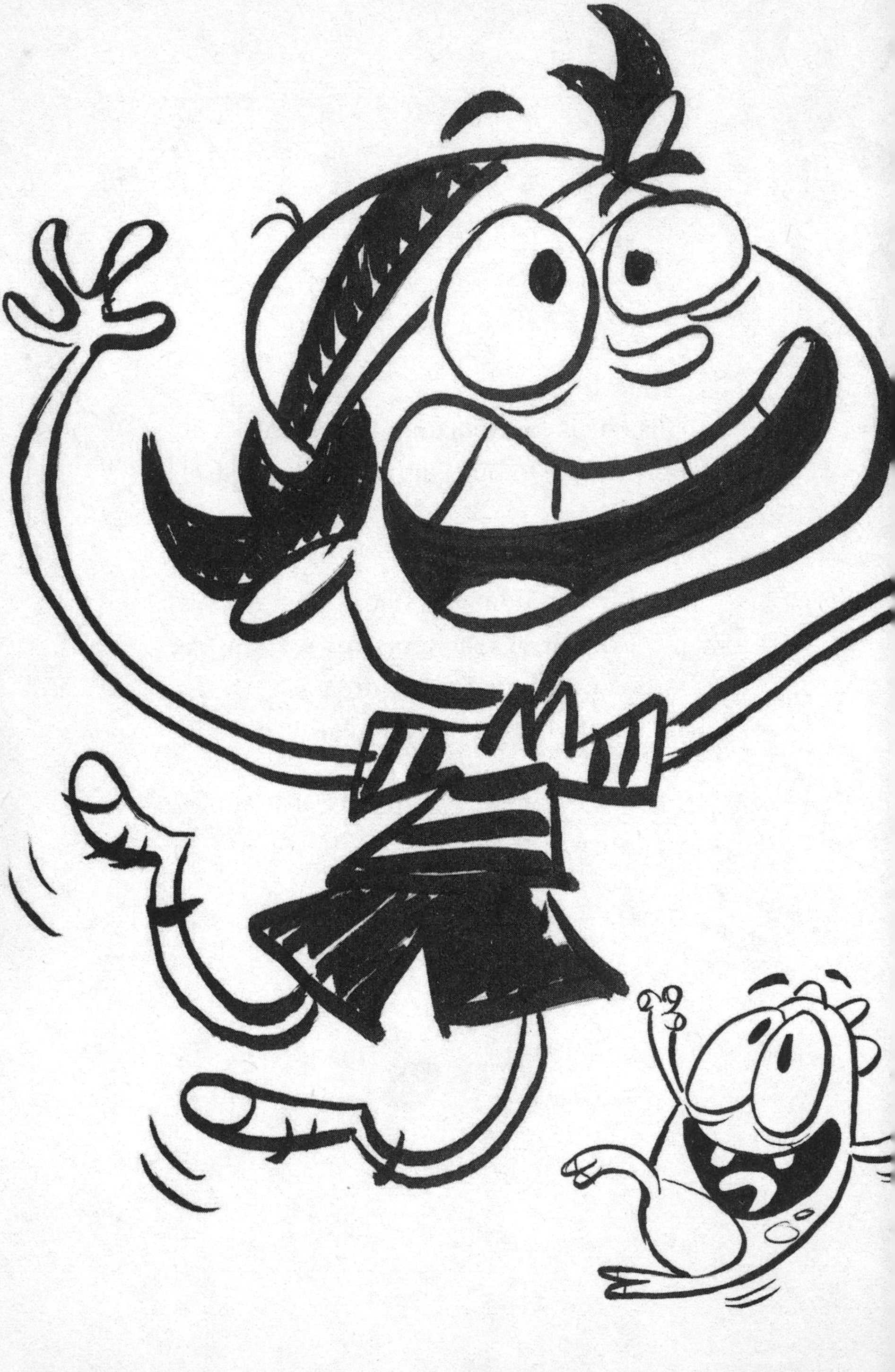

SUMMER VACATION

CHAPTER 1

Hi, I'm Harold Fuzzwonker, and today I'm visiting Fizzopolis at ten o'clock on a Monday morning. Why, you might ask, am I not at school on this fine Monday morning? Why am I walking past the Fizzopolis lagoon instead of working on some math problems for my teacher, Miss Yoobler?

Because it's SUMMER VACATION! No classes! No homework! No Miss Yoobler! And most importantly, no Garvin Snood watching my every move in class. Let me repeat, IT'S SUMMER VACATION! Okay, so obviously I'm

1

excited, and when I get VERY excited, I use ALL CAPS.

"Why is everybody meeting over there?" I asked. Floyd, my best good buddy, was sitting on my shoulder munching on a hunk of cheddar cheese. He cheese-mouth-mumbled something in my ear, but I understood him.

"I agree," I said as we passed the Ping-Pong table. "Let's go check it out. Whatever it is, it must be important. And if it's important, we need to know about it."

Floyd told me I was right, and added that we practically ran the whole place so why weren't we invited to this important gathering of Fizzies?

To say that we run the whole place might be a slight exaggeration. My dad, Dr. Fuzzwonker, actually runs Fizzopolis. Most of the time Floyd and I go to school and help out in the afternoons with Fizzy chores.

"Hey, everybody!" I yelled as I approached the gaggle of Fizzies. Nobody turned around.

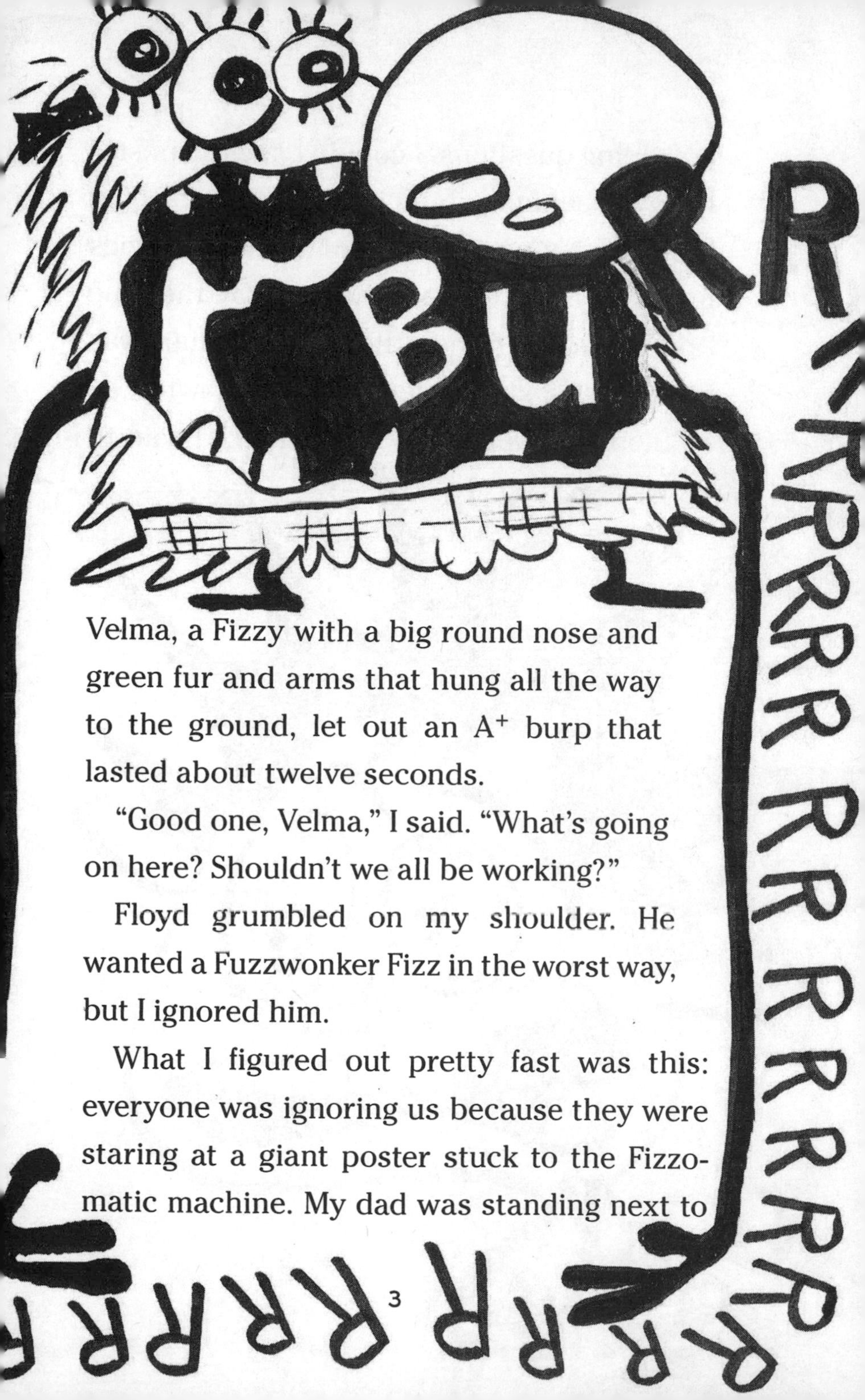
BURRRRRRR

Velma, a Fizzy with a big round nose and green fur and arms that hung all the way to the ground, let out an A+ burp that lasted about twelve seconds.

"Good one, Velma," I said. "What's going on here? Shouldn't we all be working?"

Floyd grumbled on my shoulder. He wanted a Fuzzwonker Fizz in the worst way, but I ignored him.

What I figured out pretty fast was this: everyone was ignoring us because they were staring at a giant poster stuck to the Fizzomatic machine. My dad was standing next to it, fielding questions. I couldn't see the poster hanging behind a bunch of furry Fizzies, so I pushed my way to the front. All the Fizzies fizzed as I walked past them, so by the time I popped out on the other side, my hair was totally full of static. I looked like a clown.

"Stop laughing at my weird hair," I said to Floyd.

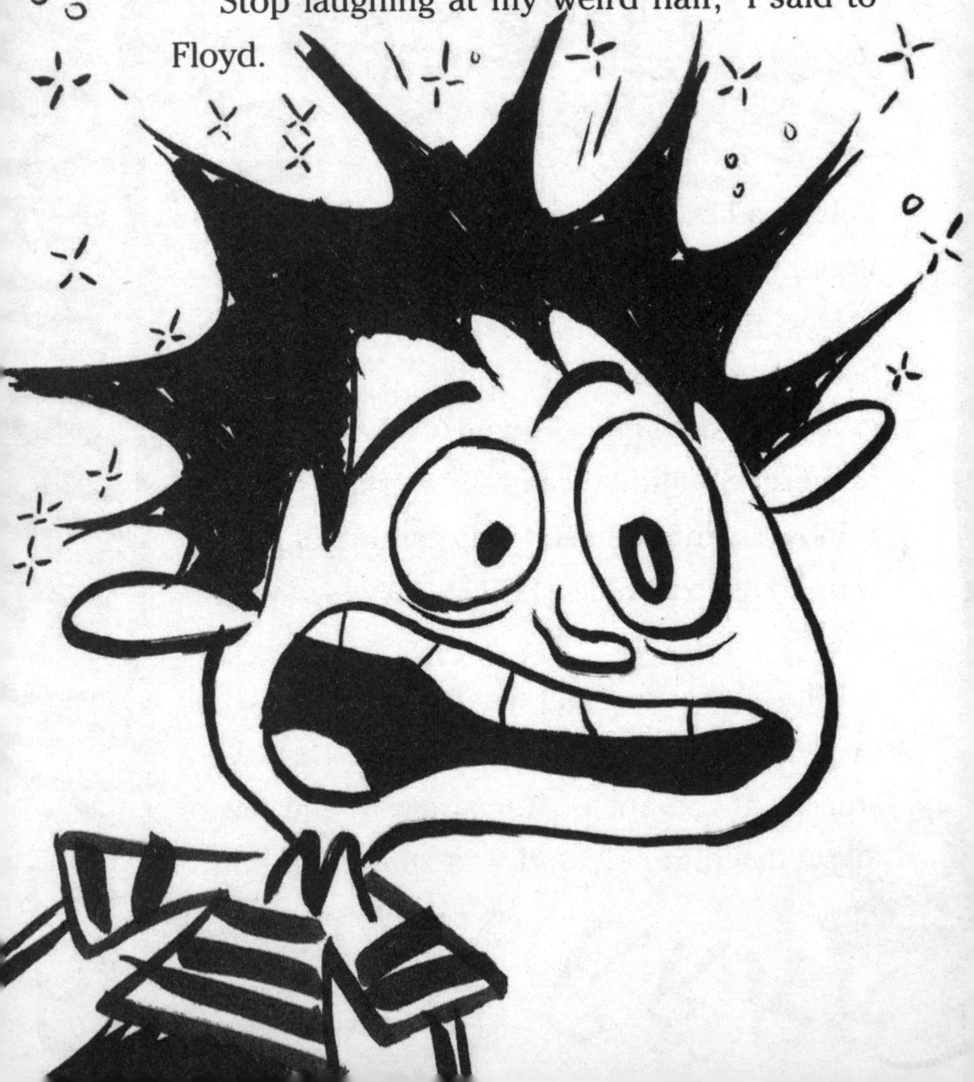

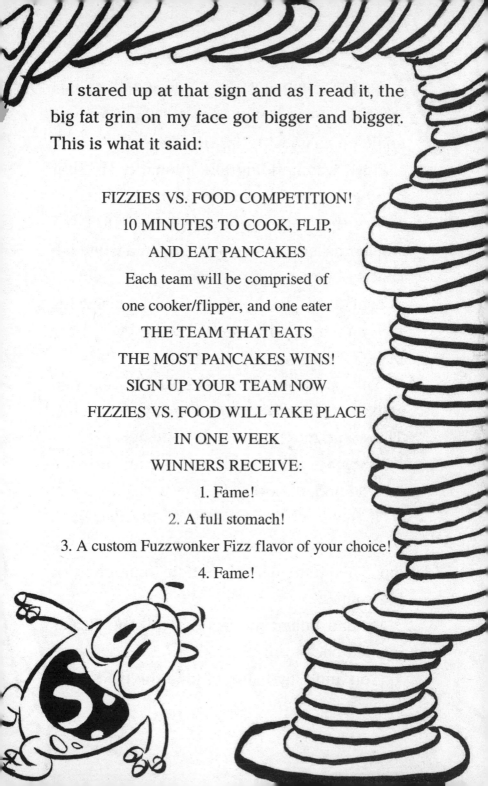

I stared up at that sign and as I read it, the big fat grin on my face got bigger and bigger. This is what it said:

FIZZIES VS. FOOD COMPETITION!
10 MINUTES TO COOK, FLIP,
AND EAT PANCAKES
Each team will be comprised of
one cooker/flipper, and one eater
THE TEAM THAT EATS
THE MOST PANCAKES WINS!
SIGN UP YOUR TEAM NOW
FIZZIES VS. FOOD WILL TAKE PLACE
IN ONE WEEK
WINNERS RECEIVE:
1. Fame!
2. A full stomach!
3. A custom Fuzzwonker Fizz flavor of your choice!
4. Fame!

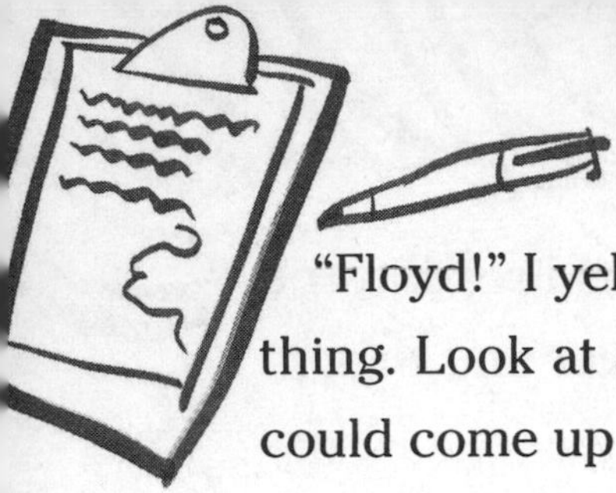

"Floyd!" I yelled. "We could totally win this thing. Look at all that fame we'd get! And we could come up with our own flavor!"

Floyd was nodding like a lunatic. My best good *eating* buddy was on board.

"Are there any more questions?" Dr. Fuzzwonker asked. He was standing in a white lab coat, holding a clipboard and a pen.

That little blowhard Grabstack raised his paw and stepped forward like he owned the place. "Could you offer a tad more fame?"

"I'm glad you asked, Grabstack," my dad said. "I'm afraid I cannot offer any more fame. There's no more room on the poster."

Grabstack looked at the poster and nodded as if he understood.

"If that's all the questions," my dad said, "let's get back to work so we can finish for the day. Then there'll be more time to practice for the contest!"

My dad pulled me aside as all the Fizzies hustled back to their jobs.

"You and Floyd should take the next week

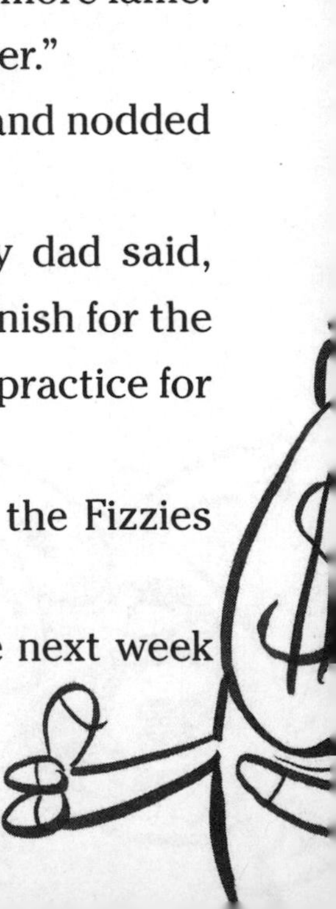

off. Consider it your paid summer vacation. Every kid needs a break."

I was thankful for the offer, but I knew my dad was giving us time off for a very different reason.

"You'd like to keep Floyd out of Fizzopolis for a week, wouldn't you?" I asked.

Floyd was high maintenance. He was always getting into mischief in Fizzopolis and making a lot of messes.

My dad tried to cover. "Who, him?" He pointed at Floyd. "Why would you say such a thing? We all love having Floyd around as much as possible."

My dad winked about nine times at me, so I got the idea. It wasn't me that needed a break from working in Fizzopolis. It was my dad who needed a break from Floyd!

"And just think, you could use this time to practice for FIZZIES VS. FOOD. You might even win!"

All that fame and our very own flavor of Fuzzwonker Fizz.

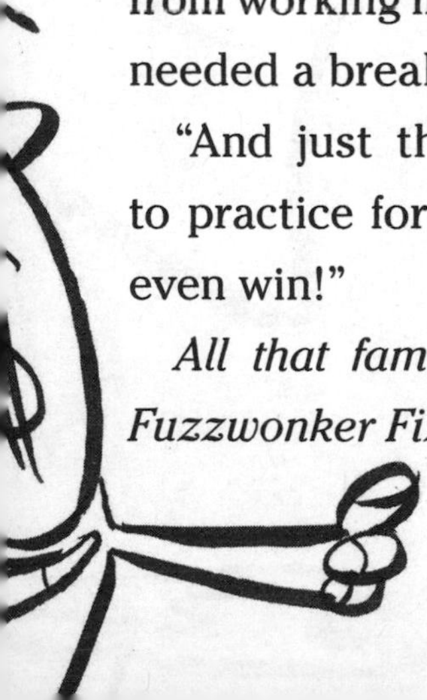

"You got a deal, Dad," I said. "We'll take the vacation."

As we headed for the elevator, I heard my dad sigh happily, like he was about to enter a day spa and have his toes pedicured.

I had it all figured out.

I would cook and flip, Floyd would eat and eat and eat. We'd have to be in perfect sync if we're going to win, and that meant practice, practice, practice.

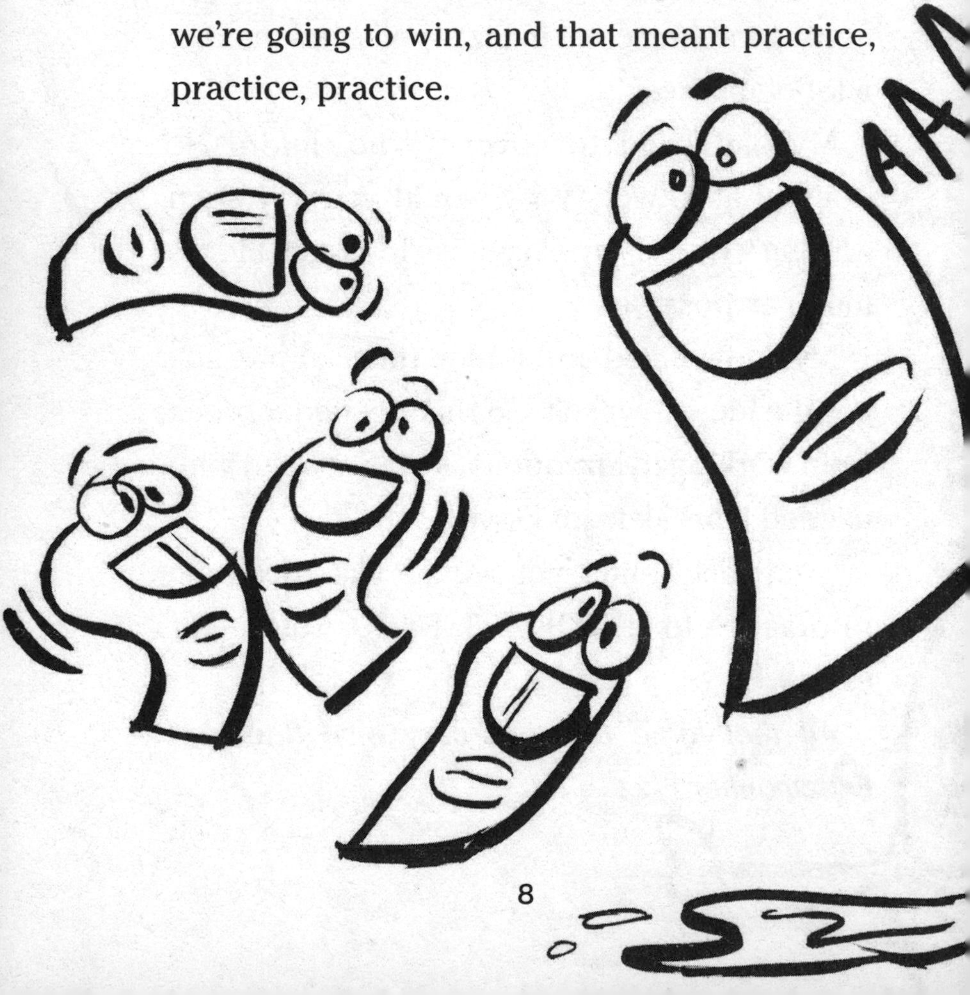

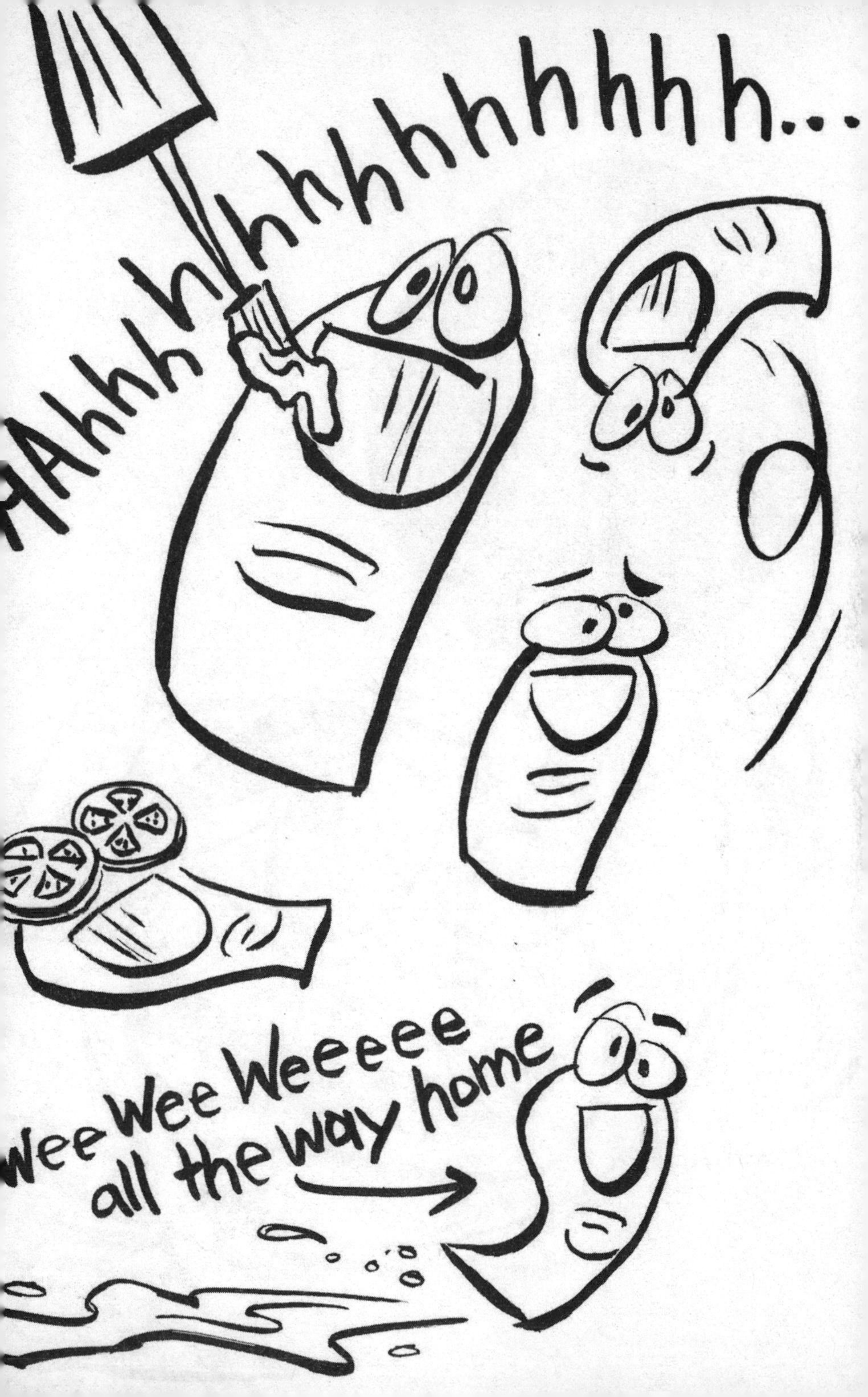
AHhhhhhhhhhhhhhhhhh...
Wee Wee Weeeee
all the way home

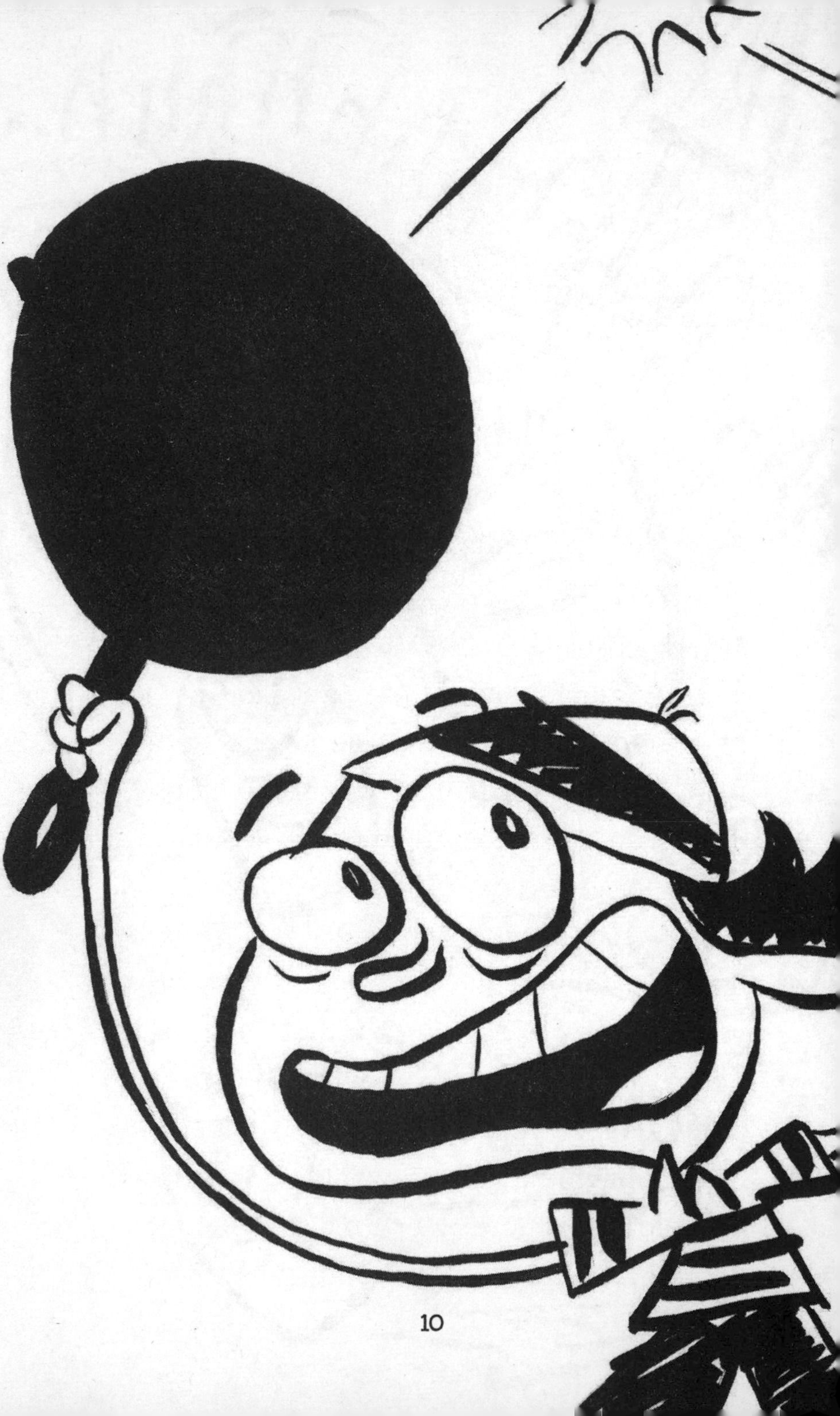

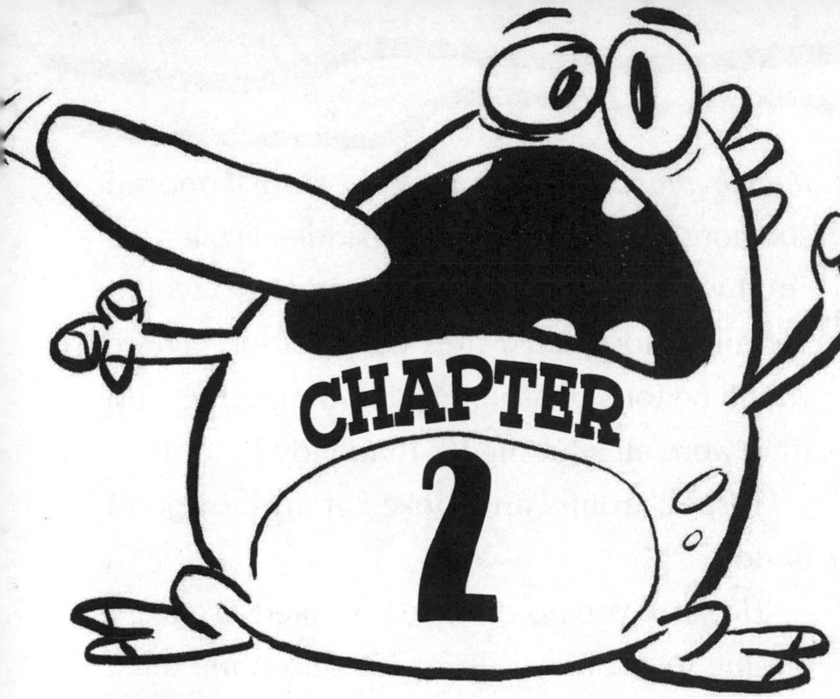
CHAPTER
2

"Number one sixteen, coming up!" I yelled. I flipped the pancake over my head and it bounced off the ceiling, took a nosedive, and landed in Floyd's open mouth. It was his 116th pancake in fourteen minutes.

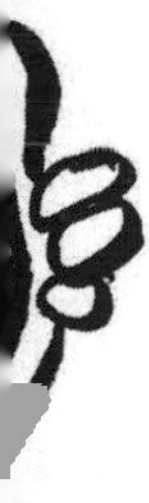

Floyd made a bunch of *munch munch munch* sounds and pounded his chest with his tiny fists. "Hit me again!" he yelled. When Floyd yells and he's not sitting on my shoulder with his head right next to my ear, it's hard to hear him. He has a very small voice, like what you might imagine a mouse would sound like if it could yell at you. Floyd made some more *munch munch munch* sounds, and I poured six more flapjacks onto the griddle. Fizzies vs. Food was only a week away, and Floyd would be going up against stiff competition. There would be tons of other Fizzies competing, and they were all a lot bigger than Floyd.

I turned around and looked at my best good buddy.

"How are you holding up?" I asked. We were hoping to get Floyd up to 150 in ten minutes. We were way short.

Floyd wobbled back and forth like he was going to pass out, then he pulled his tongue out of his head with his paw. It was dry as a bone.

"You must be parched," I said. "Let's call it a day and go work on the landing area for my jump over the house."

Floyd's tongue was lying on the counter like a piece of dried leather. The poor little dude was thirsty. Seriously, 116 pancakes will do that to a guy. I went to the refrigerator and searched for a bottle of Fuzzwonker Fizz. I looked behind a head of cabbage, but there was none there. I peeked behind the eggs and the cheese and inside the fruit crisper. No Fuzzwonker Fizz.

"That's weird," I said, scratching my head. "We've never, ever, in the history of ever, run out of Fuzzwonker Fizz."

Floyd waddled over with his gut sticking out and his tongue dragging behind him.

He jumped on my shoulder and his tongue slapped me in the back of the head.

"Could you put that thing back in your mouth?" I said. "It's gross. And dangerous."

Floyd pointed to the milk in the fridge and practically broke my eardrum. "MIIIIIIILLLLLLLLLK!"

"I wish I could give you a Fuzzwonker Fizz," I said. "In a pinch, milk will have to do."

I uncorked the milk jug and leaned the opening toward Floyd. He opened his mouth about as wide as a manhole cover and I poured the entire gallon in there. I don't know where he puts this stuff.

He burped. Milk burps are generally lame compared to Fuzzwonker Fizz burps, and this one was no exception.

Floyd asked if he could use the bathroom.

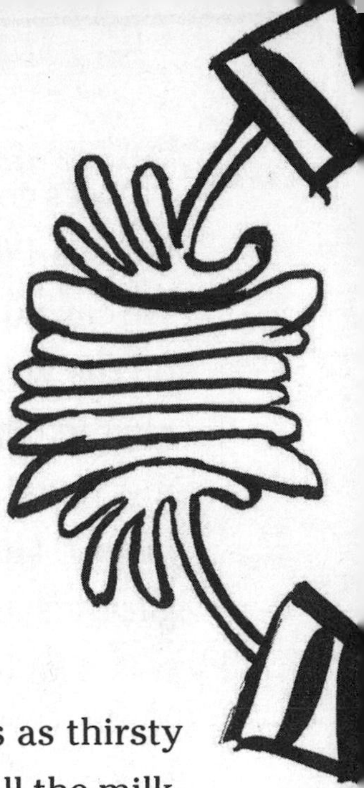

"By all means, please do," I said.

While Floyd was gone I turned off the griddle and stacked up the six pancakes he hadn't eaten. I held them like a sandwich and started munching while I took one last look inside the refrigerator for a bottle of Fuzzwonker Fizz.

Not a single bottle in there.

By the time Floyd got back I was as thirsty as he was, but he'd guzzled down all the milk. I slurped a warm glass of water from the tap and nearly barfed all over the kitchen floor.

"We need Fuzzwonker Fizz in the worst way," I said. I thought that if we went down into Fizzopolis, my dad might put us to work and cut our vacation short. "Let's go see if Sammy has any we can borrow."

Floyd is my best good buddy, and Sammy is my super-duper palomino. It's good to have both if you can get them, just in case one is out of town or has the flu or falls into a hole or something.

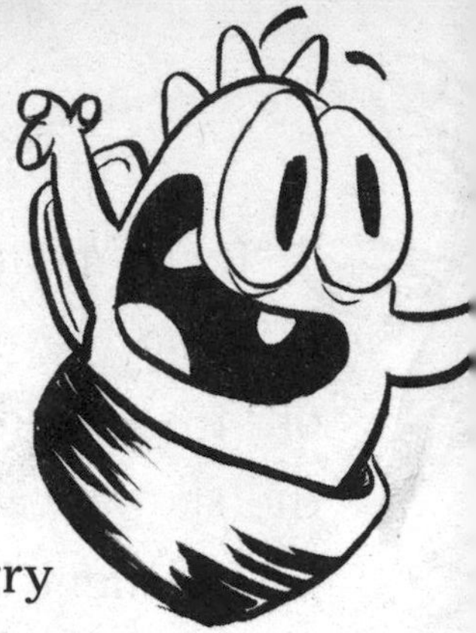

"Let's go set up my next world-famous Pflugerville bike jump. We can do some practice jumps on the way," I said as I mounted my red bike. I didn't need to carry my books around in the summer, so instead I used this nifty fanny pack I found at a garage sale. Floyd fit in there perfectly, and it was a lot lighter to carry him around. Plus, he could be right up front and open the zipper so he could see what was going on.

On the way to Sammy's I jumped over seven different things, in the following order:

A poodle.

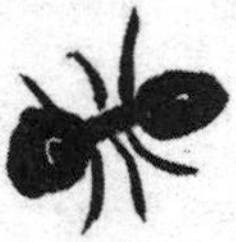

A pinecone.

An oscillating sprinkler.

A yard gnome.

A paper bag (we went back and picked it up and put it in a trash can).

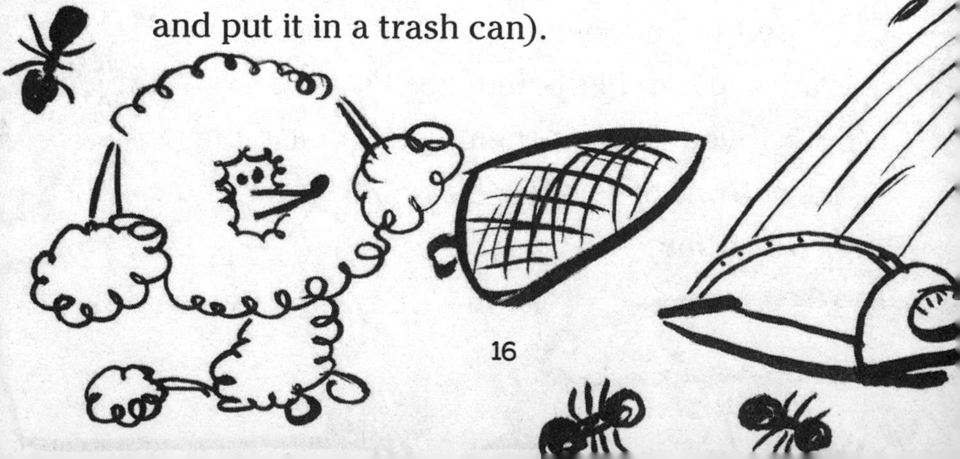

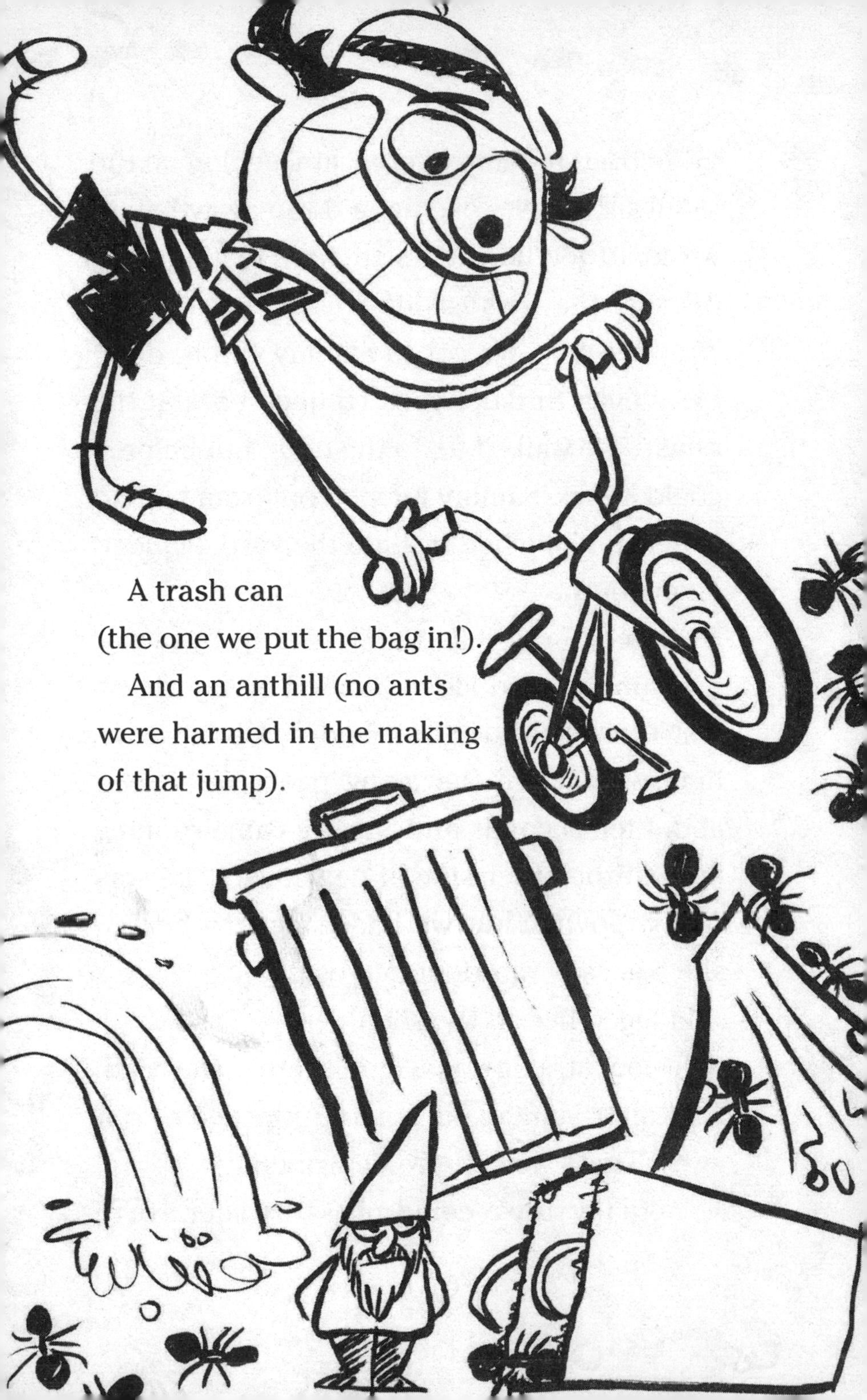

A trash can (the one we put the bag in!).

And an anthill (no ants were harmed in the making of that jump).

We tried to jump over a cat sleeping on the sidewalk, but it woke up and ran away before we could get there. Cats are hard to jump over because they're so skittish.

By the time we got to Sammy's front door, I was even thirstier than I'd been back at the house. We walked up to the door, but before I could knock, Sammy jumped out from behind a bush and pushed me into the yard. I landed on my butt.

"Gotcha!" she yelled, and then she ran away.

I stood up and Floyd jumped on my shoulder. There was no one around, so I didn't make him get back in the fanny pack. We waited about ten seconds and Sammy came running around the other side of her house. She was really moving, but we hadn't chased her, so she basically ran right into us.

I tagged her on the shoulder.

"Good strategy you got there," she said. "But after you tag me you're supposed to run away. That's how the game works."

"Actually, if we could play this later, we're

searching for a bottle of Fuzzwonker Fizz," I said. "We might die of thirst right here on your lawn if we don't get one soon."

"Come to think of it, I'm thirsty, too," Sammy said. She was out of breath from all that running. "Let's see what flavors I have. Come on."

Floyd got back inside the fanny pack, just in case Sammy's mom or dad or the little bundle of baby they had in there was awake.

"How's your little brother doing?" I asked. Her brother, Owen, wasn't even a year old.

"He tried to eat a paper cup yesterday," she said. "I don't think he's all that bright. But I like him. He cracks me up."

We arrived at the fridge and she pulled the door open. There was a bowl of potato salad in there and Floyd jumped out of my fanny pack and started attacking it.

"He just ate one hundred and sixteen pancakes," I said. "He's like a garbage disposal."

Sammy and I rummaged through her refrigerator. We explored behind the leftovers and the orange juice and the ham.

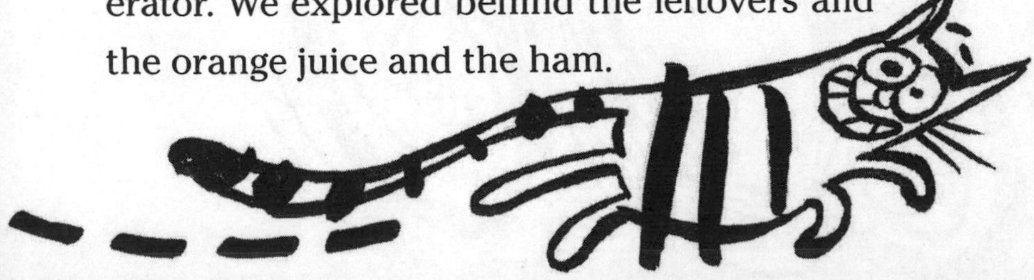

“Looks like we’re out,” she said, peering inside one more time. “Come to think of it, I haven’t had a Fuzzwonker Fizz in days.”

I just knew something was fishy. And when something’s fishy, usually the Snoods are involved.

“Come on, you guys,” I said. “Let’s go check the Pfluger Mart. There’s got to be some Fuzzwonker Fizz there.”

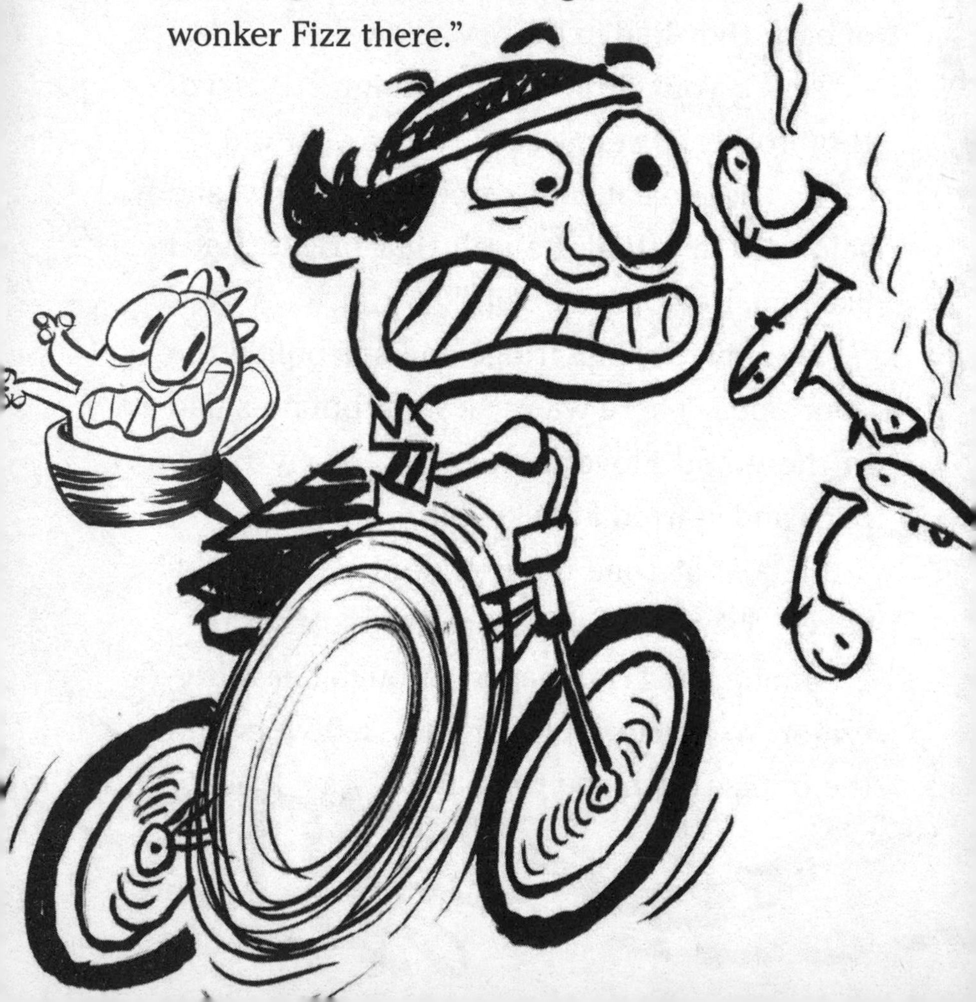

We took off on our bikes and headed for the supermarket in Pflugerville. I hardly spoke at all while we pedaled as fast as we could.

Why wasn't there any Fuzzwonker Fizz at my house or Sammy's?

Something was definitely, positively, for sure fishy!

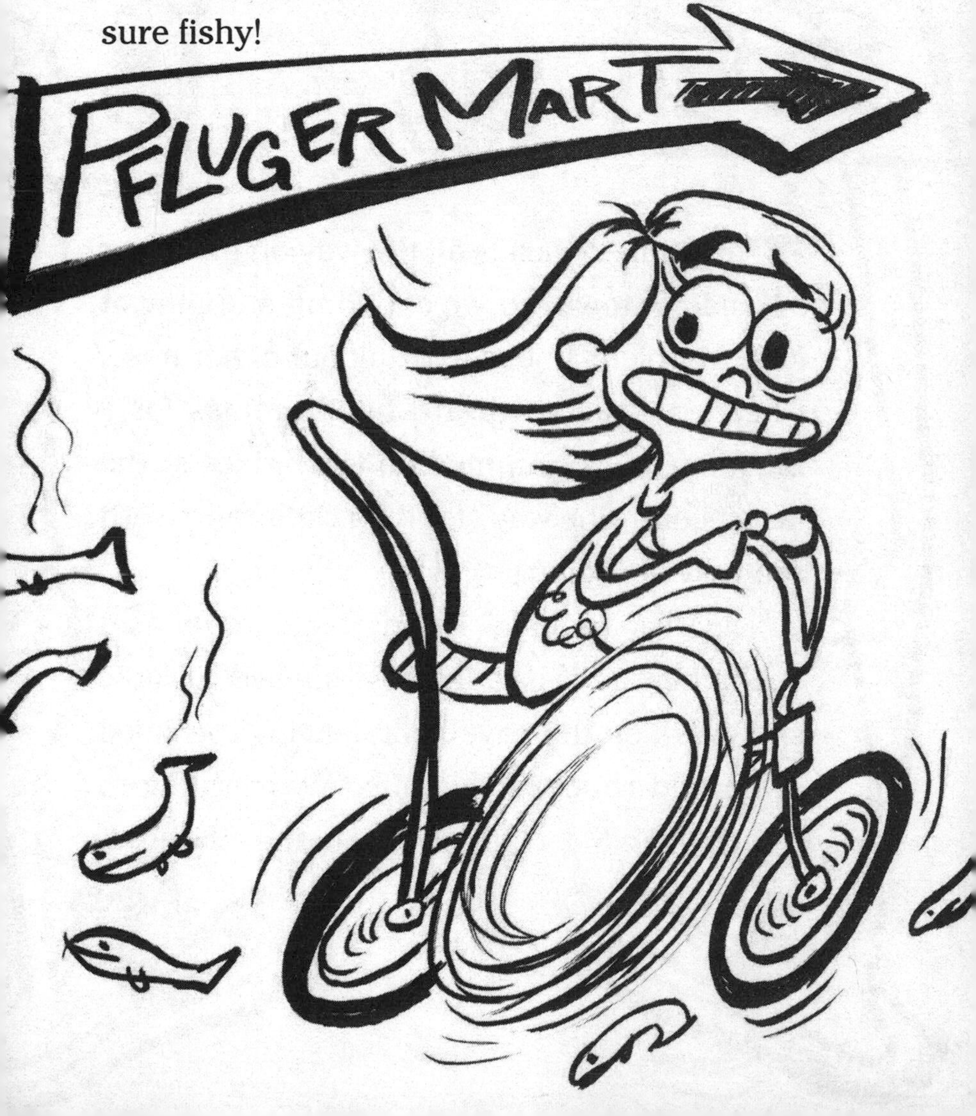
PFLUGER MART

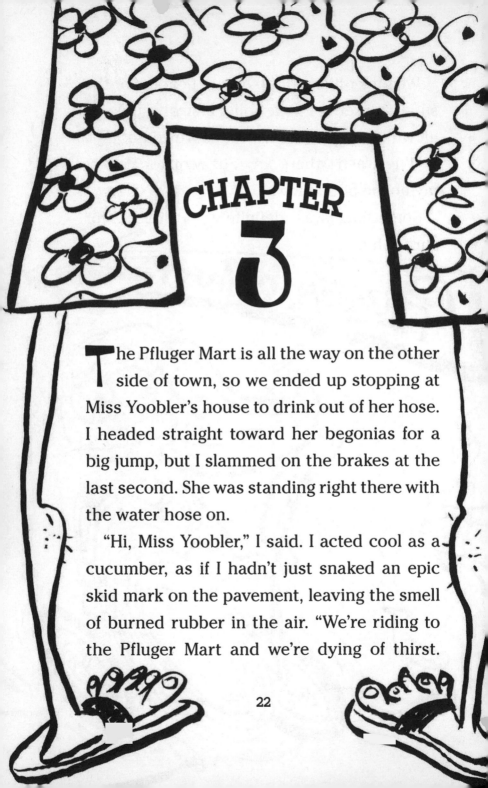

CHAPTER 3

The Pfluger Mart is all the way on the other side of town, so we ended up stopping at Miss Yoobler's house to drink out of her hose. I headed straight toward her begonias for a big jump, but I slammed on the brakes at the last second. She was standing right there with the water hose on.

"Hi, Miss Yoobler," I said. I acted cool as a cucumber, as if I hadn't just snaked an epic skid mark on the pavement, leaving the smell of burned rubber in the air. "We're riding to the Pfluger Mart and we're dying of thirst.

Any chance we could borrow your hose for a second?"

Miss Yoobler didn't turn in our direction. She kept watering the bushes by her front door.

"She has headphones on," Sammy said. "Let me try."

Sammy sucked in a huge breath of air and then went all-in: "HEY, MISS YOOOOOOO-BLER!"

Miss Yoobler didn't turn around. She was wearing crazy Bermuda shorts and a wide sun hat.

“She must really be rocking out,” I said. “I’ll go ask her.”

I got off my bike and walked through Miss Yoobler’s yard and stood behind her. Then I tapped her on the shoulder, which was a real stretch for me. She’s a lot taller than I am.

Miss Yoobler totally freaked out. She jumped about ten feet into the air, turned the hose on me, and sprayed and screamed. By the time she figured out it was just me, Miss Yoobler had drenched me from head to toe.

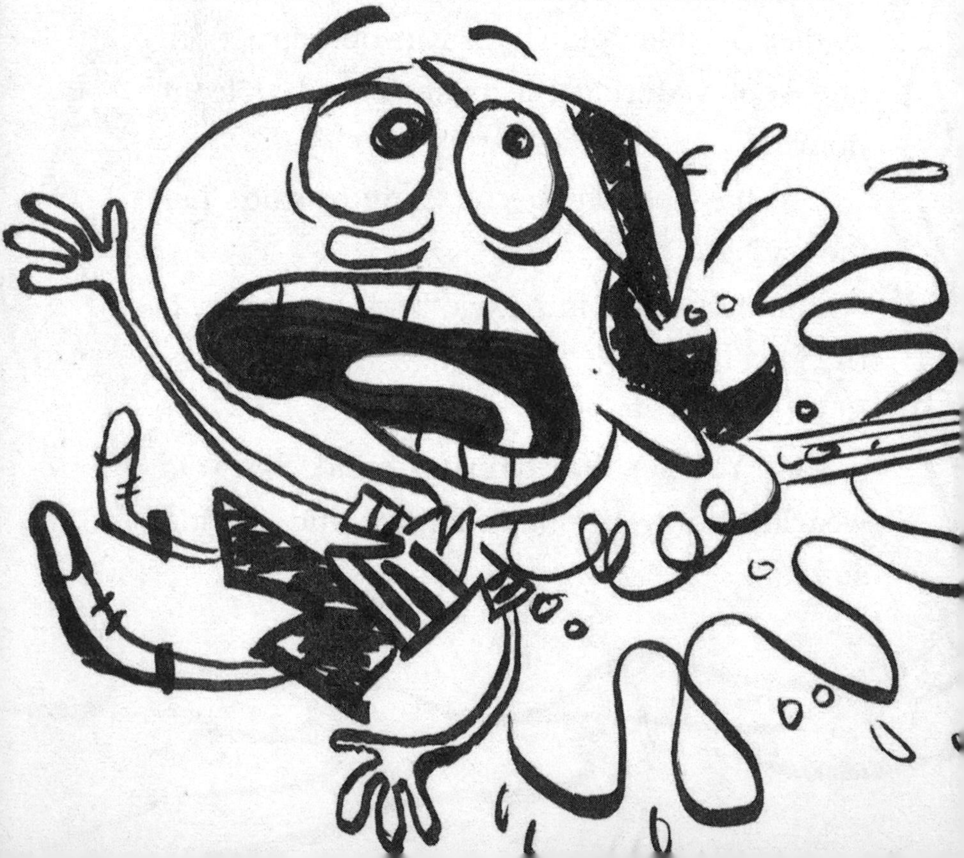

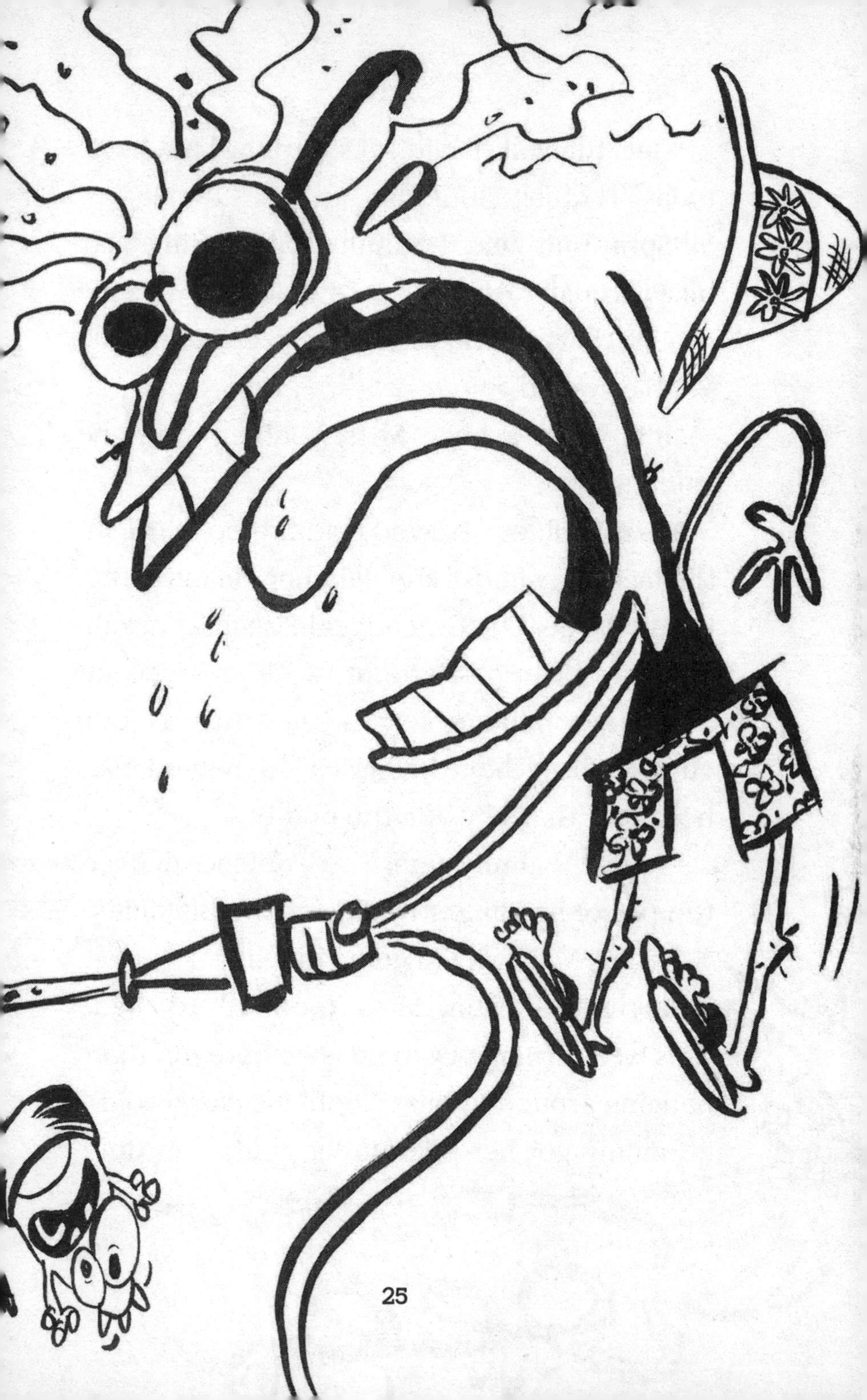

"Gee, thanks!" I said. "It's darn hot out here today. That felt fabulous."

"Spray me next!" Sammy said, riding her bike through Miss Yoobler's yard.

"Get that contraption off my grass!" Miss Yoobler yelled.

"It's called a bike, Miss Yoobler," Sammy said.

Miss Yoobler sprayed Sammy so hard in the face she almost knocked her clean off the Green Pickle. The Green Pickle is what we call Sammy's bike, on account of its green paint and green banana seat. It also has a cool chrome sissy bar that rises up behind her head, but that's beside the point.

"Whoa!" Sammy said. She wobbled all over the place, heading straight for the begonias. "Mayday, Mayday! I'm going down!"

"Spray me again, Miss Yoobler!" I yelled. This was turning out to be way more fun than hanging around in Miss Yoobler's classroom.

Sammy got her bike under control in time

to miss the flowers and circle back toward the sidewalk.

"Nice save," I said as Miss Yoobler took her headphones off. "Hi, Miss Yoobler. How's your summer going so far?"

Miss Yoobler hiked up her Bermuda shorts way past her belly button and looked down her long nose at me. Then she smiled.

"I forgot how much I enjoyed taking the summer off from all your shenanigans, Harold Fuzzwonker. Thank you for reminding me."

Then she went bananas with the hose, spraying Sammy and me until we finally got the message and continued on our journey to the Pfluger Mart.

"Have a great day, Miss Yoobler!" I yelled over my shoulder. "And thanks for the soak. We really appreciate it."

Floyd popped his head out of the fanny pack once we were out of sight and started bailing water. It was like a swimming pool in there.

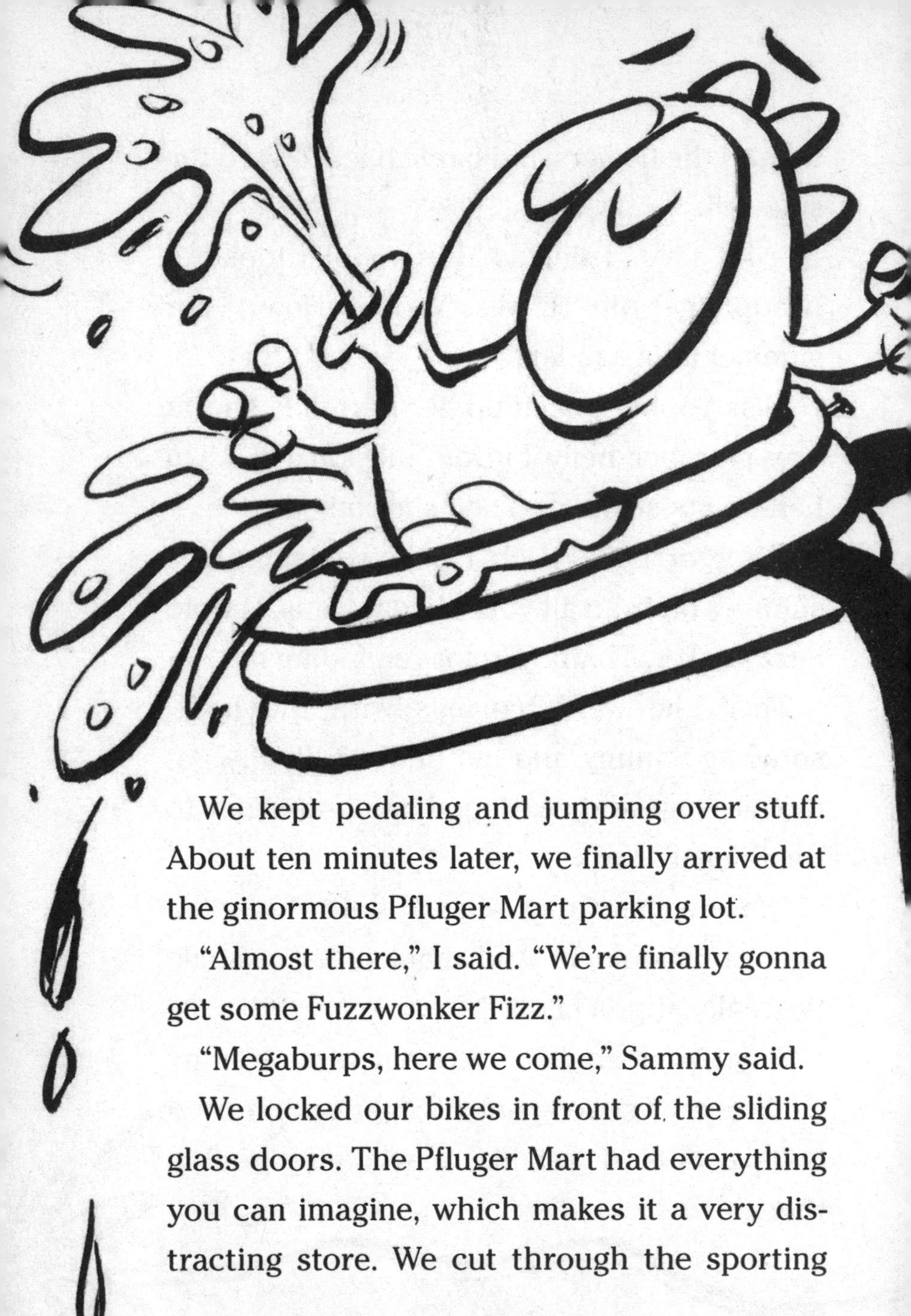

We kept pedaling and jumping over stuff. About ten minutes later, we finally arrived at the ginormous Pfluger Mart parking lot.

"Almost there," I said. "We're finally gonna get some Fuzzwonker Fizz."

"Megaburps, here we come," Sammy said.

We locked our bikes in front of the sliding glass doors. The Pfluger Mart had everything you can imagine, which makes it a very distracting store. We cut through the sporting goods department and played a game of football in aisle number eleven. Floyd got out and tried to eat some Ping-Pong balls and we chased him into the electronics section.

"Floyd," I whispered. "Be careful, little buddy. Someone might see you!"

A random kid saw Floyd running down the aisle and tried to grab him. "Mom! I want *that* toy!"

The little runt chased Floyd all the way around a corner and then gave up.

"This is getting out of hand fast," I said to Sammy. "We need to find that Fuzzwonker Fizz and hightail it."

"You go thataway," Sammy said, pointing down the aisle. "I'll come around the other side and we'll trap Floyd on the next aisle over."

"Good plan."

I crept forward quietly because Floyd only got rowdier if I chased him. When I turned the corner I saw him standing in the middle of aisle seventeen, staring up at the Legos.

Sammy came around the corner at the other end of the toy section, and we both moved forward with our arms out.

Floyd was so mesmerized by all the toys he didn't even see us coming.

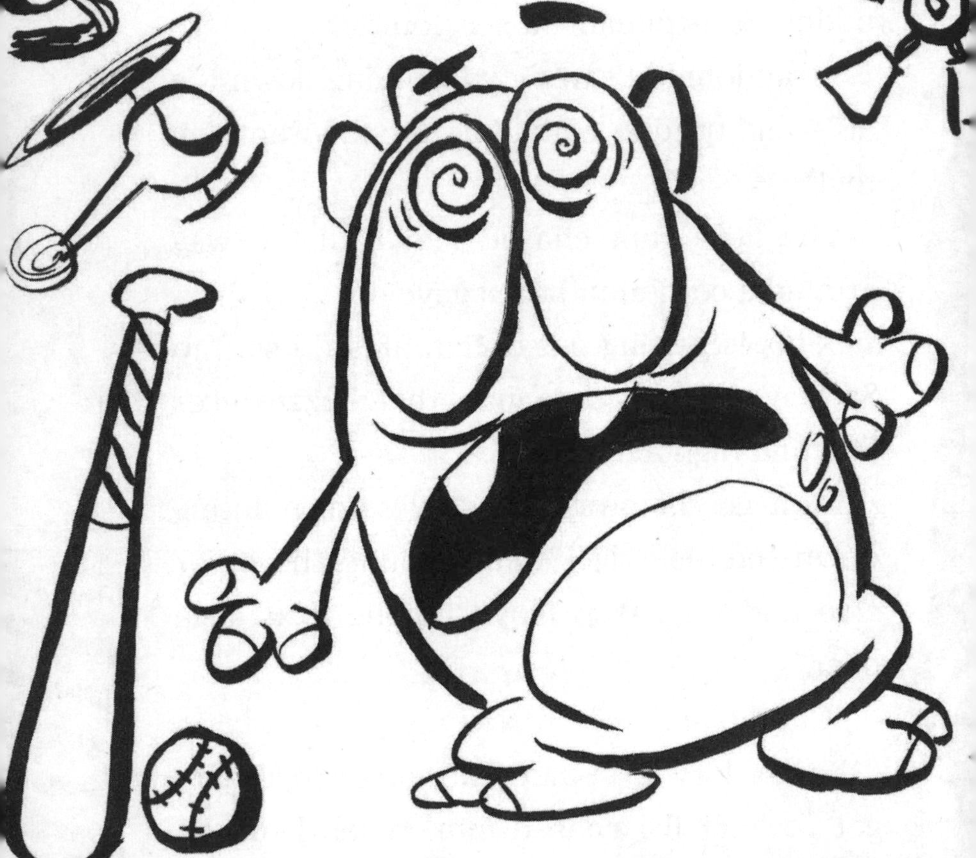

"Gotcha!" I said. I held Floyd's face right up next to mine and gave him my stern look.

"You're my best good buddy, but you can't run around the Pfluger Mart like that. What if someone sees you?"

"Someone already did," Sammy said. The little kid was back and he was pointing at Floyd. I turned around and stuffed Floyd in my fanny pack and started walking double time.

"He took the toy I want!" the little brat cried again.

Once I turned the corner I full-on sprinted toward the grocery department and nearly slid headfirst into a giant candy display.

"Whew, close call."

The towering stacks of product in front of me went all the way to the ceiling. Kids were grabbing packages one right after the other. Sammy walked

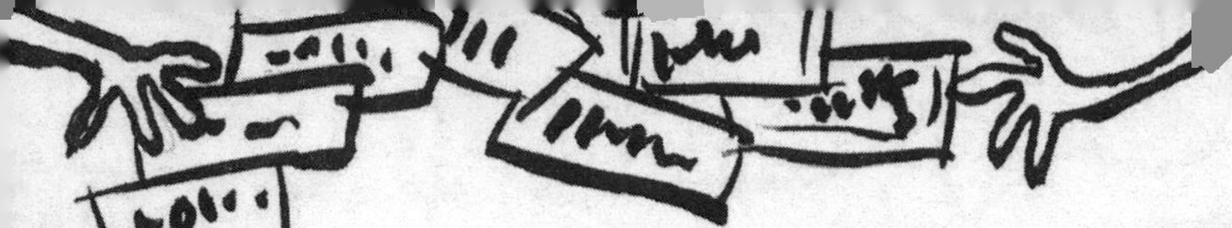

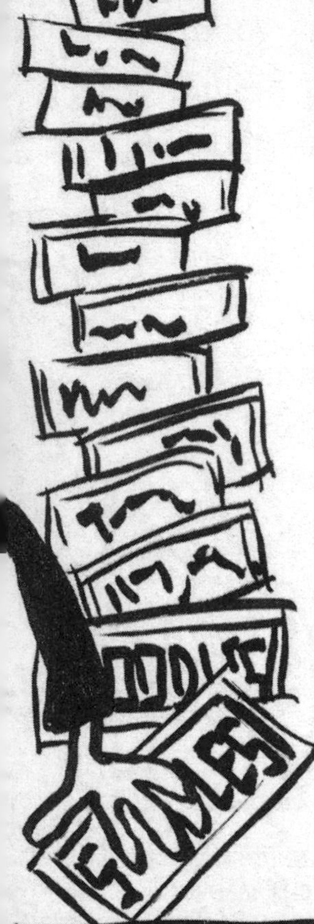

up and we both grabbed one of the items.

"Snoodles?" I said. "What the heck is a Snoodle?"

Some kid in a striped shirt and flip-flops laughed in my face. "What's a *Snoodle*? Are you nuts! It's only the best candy in the world. Where have you been?"

I couldn't tell him I'd been locked in my house feeding pancakes to a little green creature.

The Snoodles package was yellow with blocky red letters. It was the most boring packaging I'd ever seen.

"There's only one company that

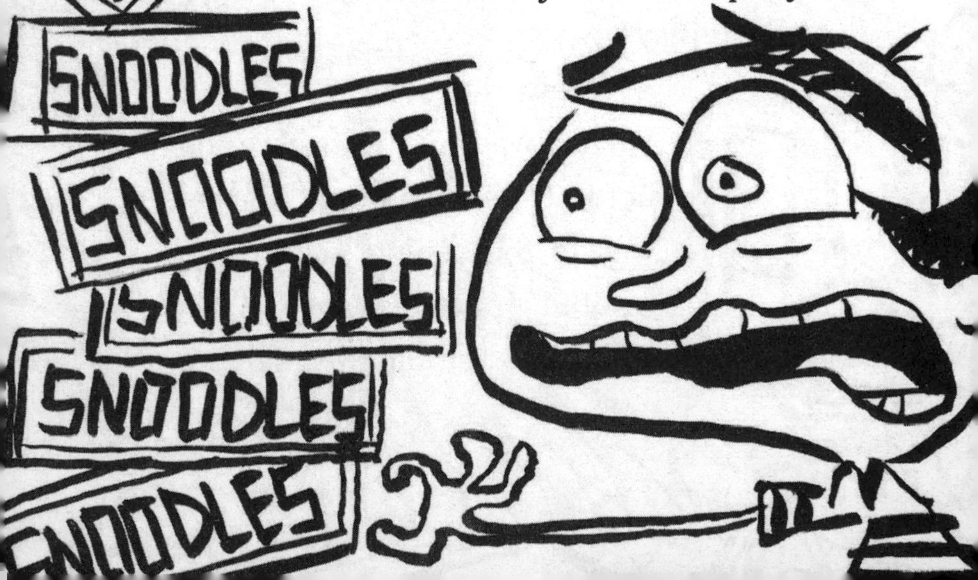
SNOODLES
SNOODLES
SNOODLES
SNOODLES

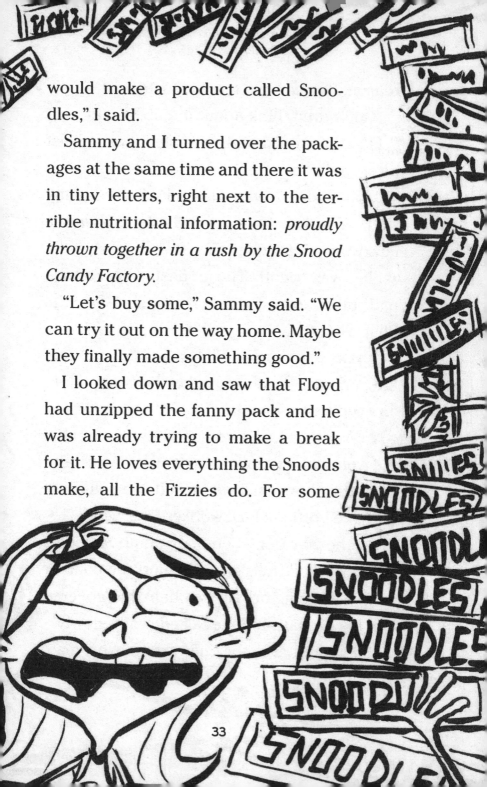

would make a product called Snoodles," I said.

Sammy and I turned over the packages at the same time and there it was in tiny letters, right next to the terrible nutritional information: *proudly thrown together in a rush by the Snood Candy Factory.*

"Let's buy some," Sammy said. "We can try it out on the way home. Maybe they finally made something good."

I looked down and saw that Floyd had unzipped the fanny pack and he was already trying to make a break for it. He loves everything the Snoods make, all the Fizzies do. For some

33

reason, Fizzies have terrible taste.

"Don't even think about it, bub," I said.

Floyd mumbled and grumbled, but at least he stayed put.

"You know, I was just thinking," Sammy said. "The last time I was here, this was a Fuzzwonker Fizz display."

She was right! Those dastardly Snoods had taken over prime real estate at the Pfluger Mart.

"Let's keep looking," I said. "They must have moved the Fuzzwonker Fizz display to an even better location."

We searched and searched and searched. We went up and down every aisle. Twice! But no matter how hard we looked, we could not find one bottle of Fuzzwonker Fizz.

On the way out to buy our dumb Snoodles candy I asked the slacker behind the counter what was going on. He had hair that covered half his eyeballs and he talked really slowly.

"Snoodles are the newest craze, man. They're rad."

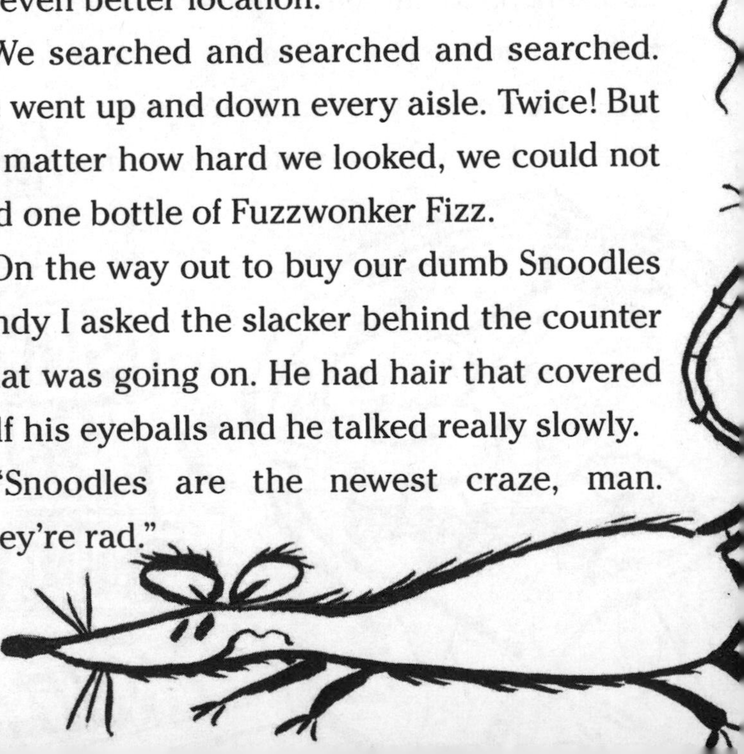

"Okaaaaaay," Sammy said. "But where's all the Fuzzwonker Fizz?"

The cashier shrugged and handed us our change. "We've been back-ordered on Fuzz-wonker Fizz for days. It's like there's some kind of shortage or something. Rad fanny pack, man. Those things are making a come-back."

It was nice that the cashier noticed my cool fanny pack, but it didn't stop me from thinking something big was going on here.

I looked at the Snoodles candy in my hand and narrowed my eyes. "I smell a rat."

"We don't sell rats here," the cashier said in his slow drawl. He pointed out the door. "Pflugerville Pet World has them. That way."

I rolled my eyes and headed for the door.

"Come on, Sammy. We need to figure out what the heck is happening to all the Fuzz-wonker Fizz in this town."

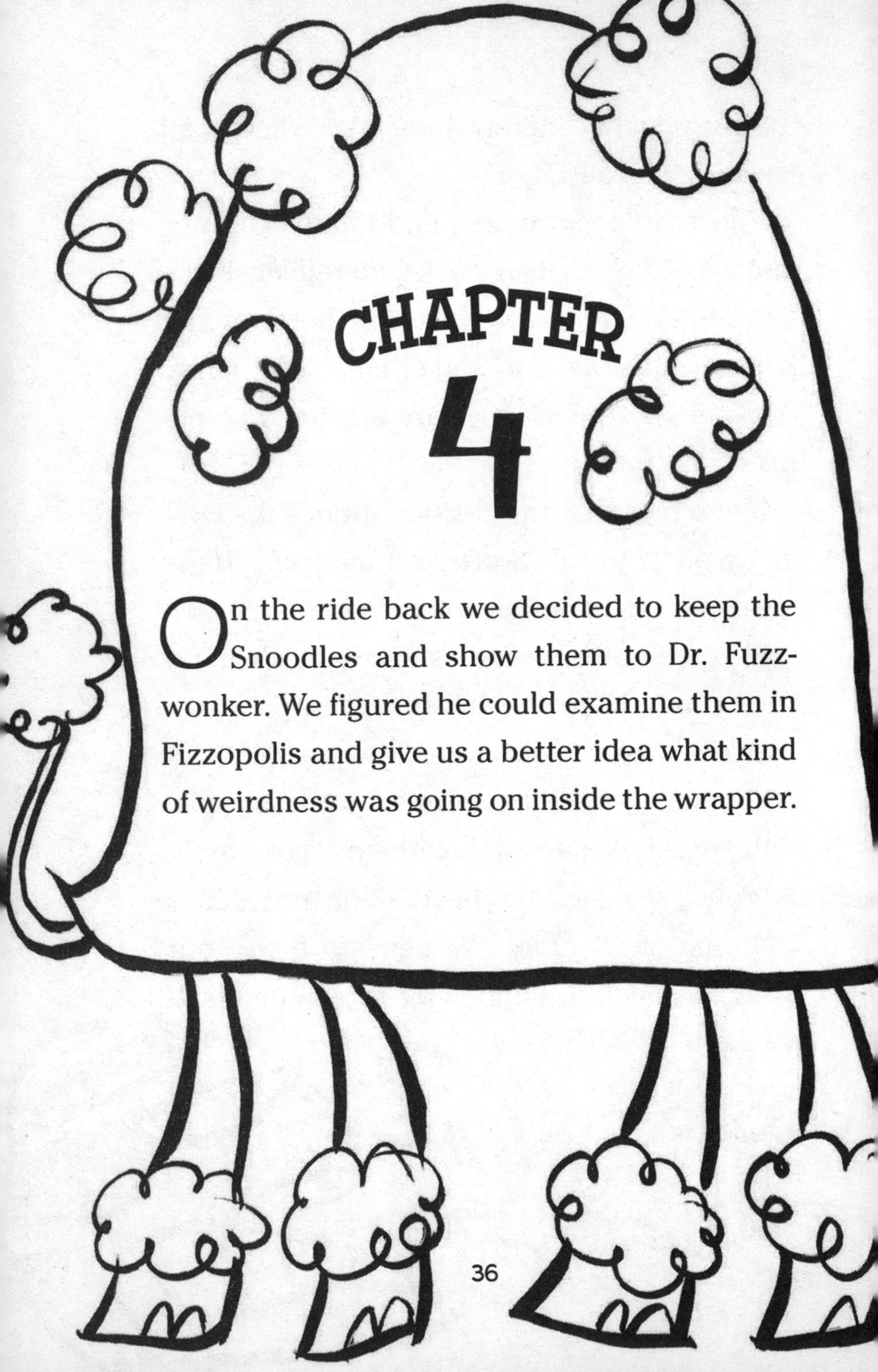

CHAPTER 4

On the ride back we decided to keep the Snoodles and show them to Dr. Fuzzwonker. We figured he could examine them in Fizzopolis and give us a better idea what kind of weirdness was going on inside the wrapper.

We stopped at Miss Yoobler's place and let her hose us down again, and I asked her if I could jump over her begonias. She told me if I did, she'd make sure I got sent back to the first grade and stayed there for twelve thousand years.

"But I'm way older than that!" I complained.

She let her giant dog out of her house and it chased us down the street. She called it a mastadoodle, which apparently is a cross between a poodle and the biggest dog in the world. It barely fit through her front door, but it was as slow as a turtle. We outran it easy on our bikes.

The sun dried off our clothes again and

we raced through the neighborhood, into my house, and down the elevator into Fizzopolis. On the way Floyd got on my shoulder where he likes it best and told me we were retiring the fanny pack.

"It's like a sardine can in there," he said into my ear.

When the doors opened at the bottom of the elevator shaft, all three of our jaws dropped.

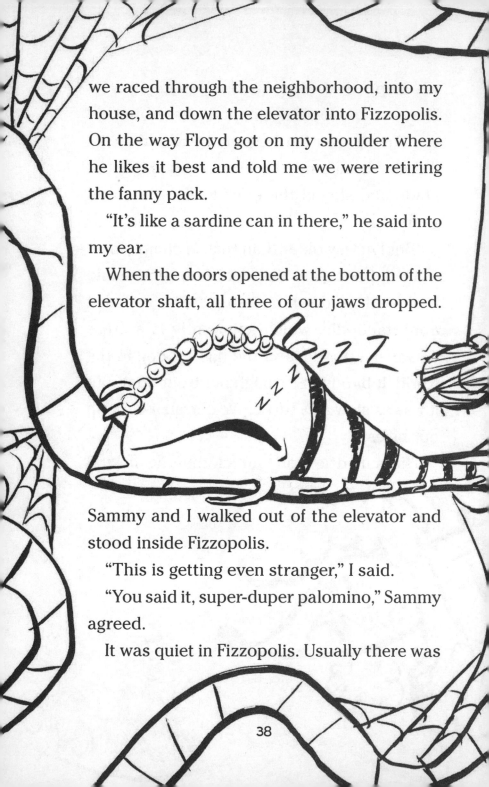

Sammy and I walked out of the elevator and stood inside Fizzopolis.

"This is getting even stranger," I said.

"You said it, super-duper palomino," Sammy agreed.

It was quiet in Fizzopolis. Usually there was

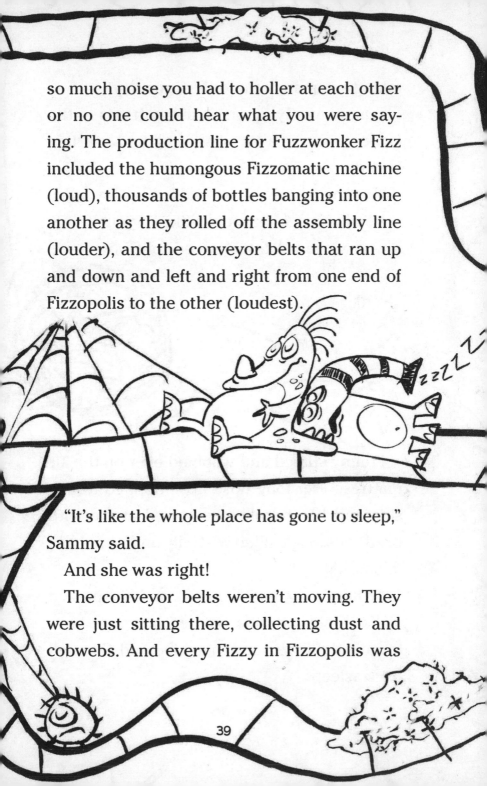

so much noise you had to holler at each other or no one could hear what you were saying. The production line for Fuzzwonker Fizz included the humongous Fizzomatic machine (loud), thousands of bottles banging into one another as they rolled off the assembly line (louder), and the conveyor belts that ran up and down and left and right from one end of Fizzopolis to the other (loudest).

"It's like the whole place has gone to sleep," Sammy said.

And she was right!

The conveyor belts weren't moving. They were just sitting there, collecting dust and cobwebs. And every Fizzy in Fizzopolis was taking a nap. In the middle of the day!

Franny was lying on an air mattress in the lagoon, making a lot of snoring and snarfing sounds.

"Franny!" I said as we walked by. My voice echoed through Fizzopolis like I'd yelled over a vast canyon. A tumbleweed rolled by.

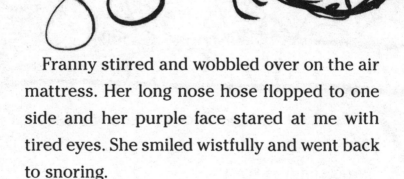

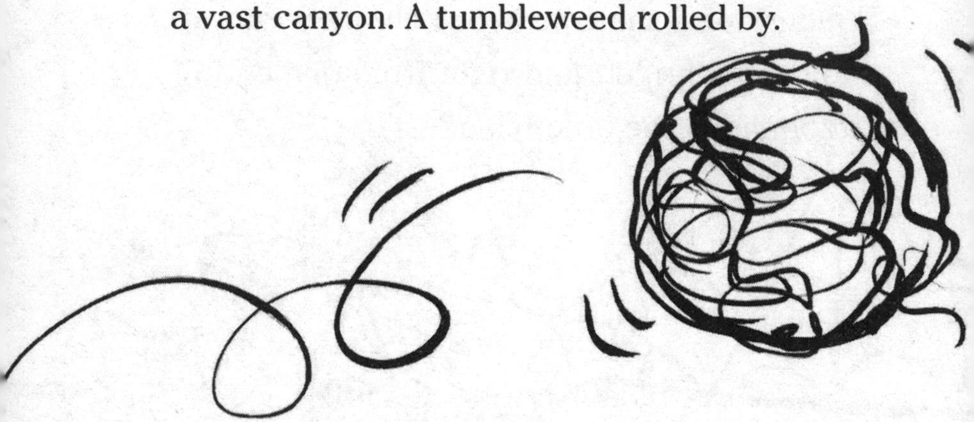

Franny stirred and wobbled over on the air mattress. Her long nose hose flopped to one side and her purple face stared at me with tired eyes. She smiled wistfully and went back to snoring.

"Where's my dad?" I asked, and she perked up for a second. She pointed her nose hose toward the Fizzomatic machine and then fell back asleep.

We walked past Fizzy after Fizzy and they were all taking afternoon naps. George, who was the size of a sofa and shaped like one too, was snoozing right next to his rubber ducky. His soft, yellow fur moved up and down as his breath rumbled quietly.

"It's like a spell has been cast over Fizzopolis," Sammy said. "We better hurry!"

She didn't have to tell me twice. I ran by the tumbleweed and wished for the hundredth time that I had a Fuzzwonker Fizz. We found my dad sitting on the ground with his back leaned up against the Fizzomatic machine.

"Dr. Fuzzwonker," Sammy said. She approached him slowly like he was an injured dog that might jump up and start barking in her face. Sammy was good with dogs and distraught food scientists. "Can you tell us what's going on?"

Dr. Fuzzwonker was clutching a bottle of Fuzzwonker Fizz, staring at it longingly, like it was the last bottle in the known universe.

"This is the last bottle of Fuzzwonker Fizz in

the known universe," he said. I guess I know my dad even better than I thought.

"But that's impossible," I said.

Floyd jumped high off my shoulder. He twisted and spun and went into a nosedive like a kamikaze pilot.

"You better hold on to that Fuzzwonker Fizz," Sammy told my dad.

Floyd landed on the bottle and

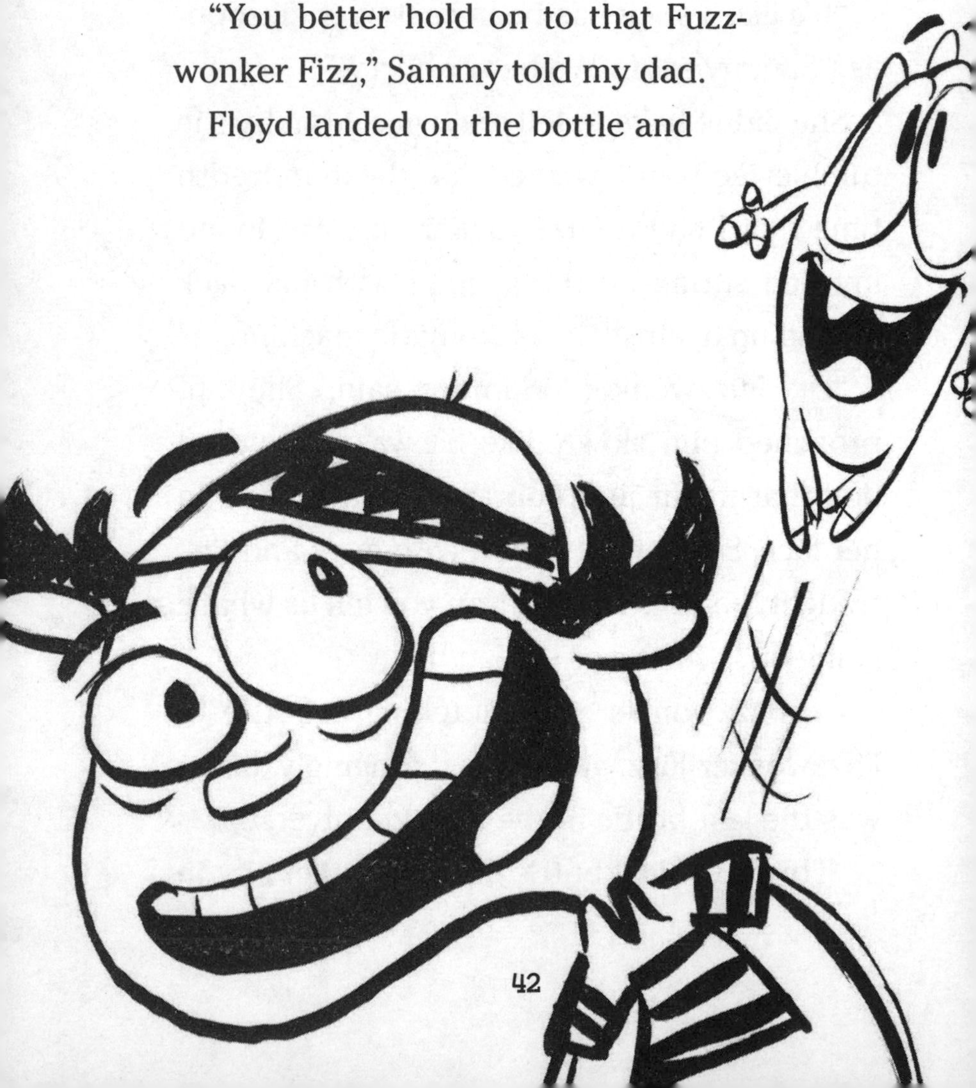

wrapped both arms and legs around it. My dad popped the top anyway and tipped the contents into his mouth. Floyd went along for the ride, and then Dr. Fuzzwonker set the bottle down and Floyd drank what was left. Then he licked the bottle.

My dad let out a sad thirteen-second burp, then Floyd started crying and burping and hiccupping.

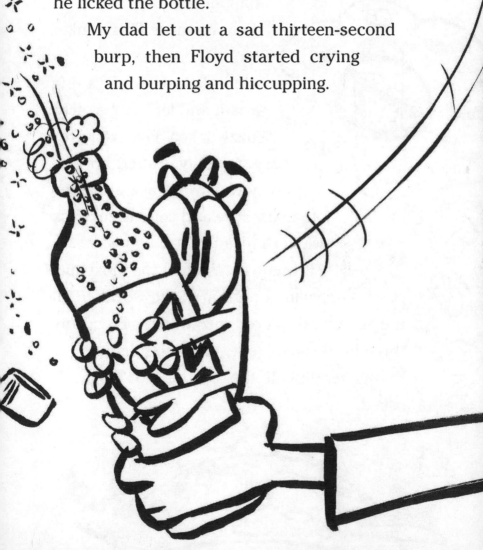

"It's okay, you guys," I said. I felt terrible. Maybe I've already drank my last Fuzzwonker Fizz, and I'll never burp like a maniac again! Saddest. Thought. Ever.

I sat down next to Dr. Fuzzwonker. "What happened, Dad? Why is there no more Fuzzwonker Fizz?"

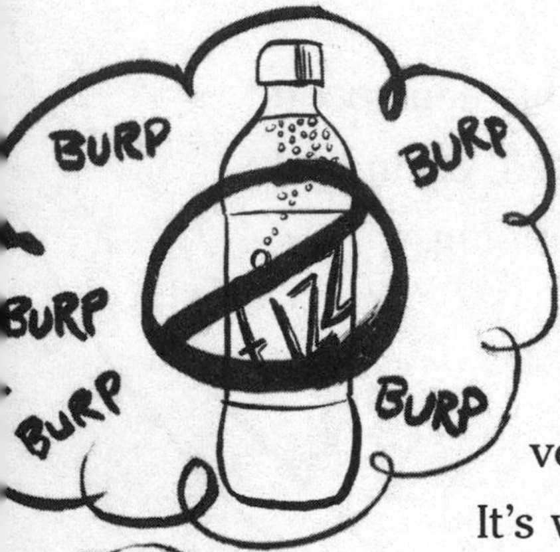
BURP
BURP
BURP
BURP
BURP
FIZZ

My dad drew in a big breath and let it out slowly. "Fuzzwonker Fizz requires very carefully crafted bottles. It's why we always ask everyone to make sure and send them back when they finish."

It was true. We had the most successful recycling program in the world. In all the time we'd offered Fuzzwonker Fizz, only three bottles had gone out of circulation.

"Where did all the bottles go?" Sammy asked.

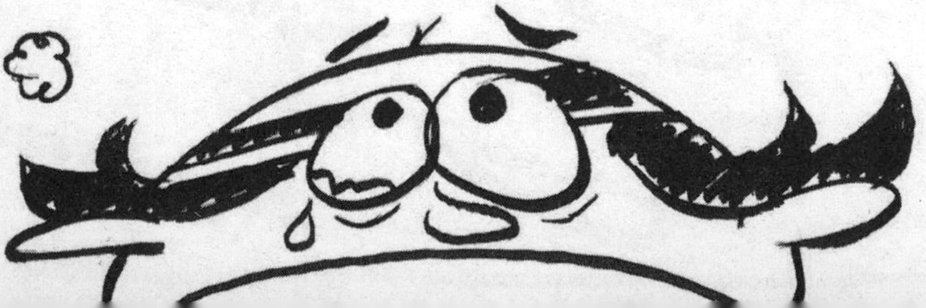

Dr. Fuzzwonker stood up and looked at the amazing Fizzomatic machine. "That's just it—I have no idea. We've been getting fewer and fewer bottles over the past few weeks, but I didn't want to alarm you. I haven't seen a bottle come back in six days. They're all gone."

"How many bottles are we talking about here?" I asked.

Dr. Fuzzwonker pointed to a display on the Fizzomatic machine with red numbers. There was a column for bottles that were in production. It had a big fat zero under it. Another column was called bottles in circulation. That one had a really big number under it.

"One hundred thousand bottles!" I said.

BOTTLES
IN PRODUCTION
IN CIRCULATION
0
100,000

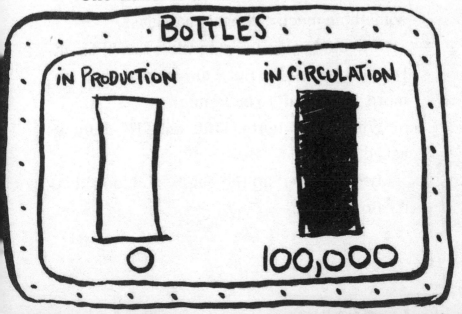

"That's enough Fuzzwonker Fizz for everyone in Pflugerville times ten!"

"Why can't you just make more bottles?" Sammy asked.

"Yeah," I agreed. "Let's make more. We can do this. The Fizzies will help us."

Dr. Fuzzwonker shook his head miserably. "Those bottles are made of a special material. It's not just any bottle that can hold the fizzy power of a Fuzzwonker Fizz! And we've long since run out of the stuff we need to make more bottles."

Floyd got all bummed out and threw the one bottle we had against the Fizzomatic machine. It bounced off the iron hull like it was made of something much stronger than glass.

"If I could make more bottles, I would," Dr. Fuzzwonker said. "But I'm afraid there's no more bottle stuff to be found."

"What's this bottle stuff called?" Sammy asked.

My dad picked up the empty and looked at it. "Bottle Stuff."

Sometimes my dad came up with great names for things, and sometimes he came up with names like Bottle Stuff.

"Someone must be hoarding bottles made of Bottle Stuff," Sammy said. Sammy was like a private detective. She was always figuring things out before anyone else.

"You may be right," my dad agreed, perking up a little.

Floyd crawled up my leg and climbed into the fanny pack. He milled around in there for a while and then came back out holding the package of Snoodles.

"Oh yeah," Sammy said. "I forgot about my Snoodles."

Sammy pulled hers out of her back pocket. It was smashed like a pancake. Floyd and Sammy started munching at the same time.

Munch munch munch.

They both got strange looks on their faces at the same time.

"It tastes that bad, huh?" I said.

Sammy opened her mouth to talk, and

burp

before she could tell us how yuck-city Snoodles were, she let out a tiny little burp.

"I think it was orange flavor," she said. "But
it might have been tutti-frutti."

Then Floyd burped. It was also a teensy-
weensy burp.

"Stop eating, you guys!" I said. The whole
situation was becoming clear. "The Snoods
are up to no good. They must have something
to do with all our missing bottles."

"Say, you might be right," my dad said.

"These Snoodles seem to be causing some unusual side effects that bear some resemblance to Fuzzwonker Fizz."

I took the rest of Sammy's Snoodle, but Floyd ate his before I could get my hands on it.

"Here, Dad," I said. "You examine this sample. We'll go see what we can find out in Pflugerville."

"Good plan," Dr. Fuzzwonker said. He took the Snoodle sample with a pair of tweezers and smiled for the first time since we'd arrived in Fizzopolis. Scientists are always happy when they have something to figure out.

Floyd jumped on my shoulder and I turned to Sammy.

"Come on, guys. We need to find those bottles and get this assembly line working again! And I know the first place we need to look."

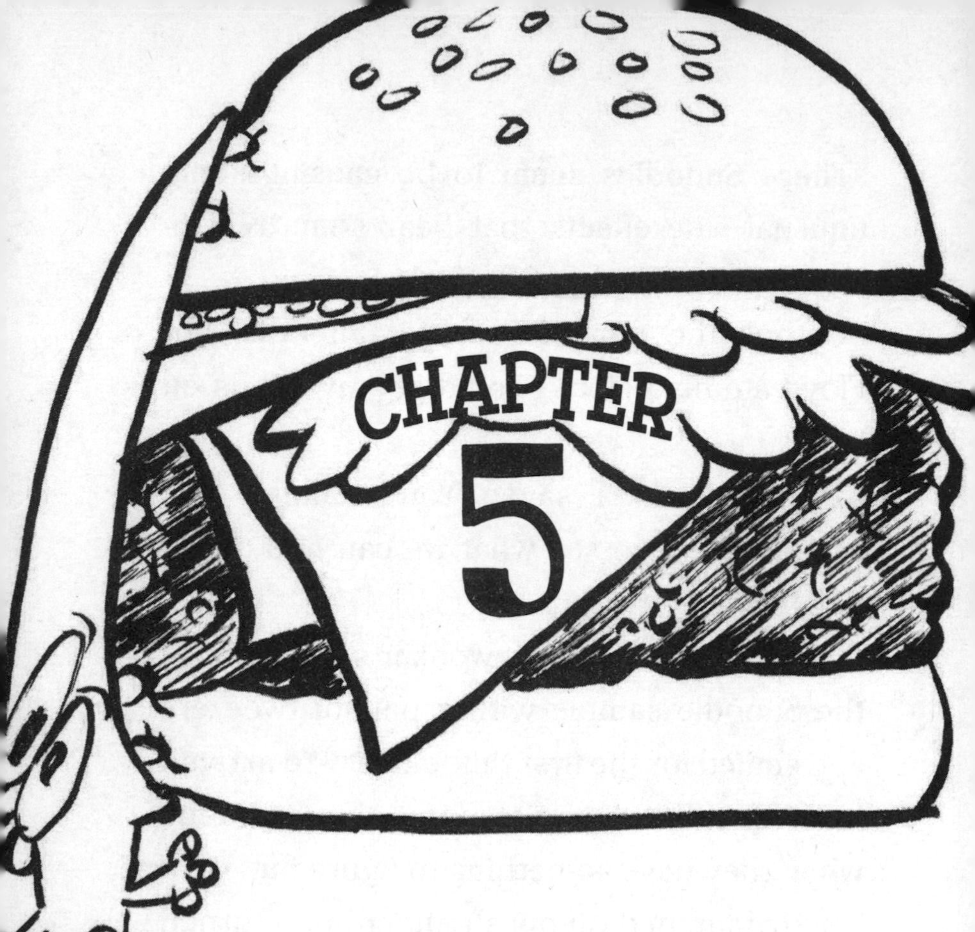

CHAPTER 5

Floyd was hungry as usual, so we stopped off at the Pflugerville Hamburger Shack on the way to our investigation of Snoodles. We all ordered Pfluger burgers with fries and milk shakes.

After finding a quiet booth in the corner, I dropped Floyd's lunch into my backpack.

"Here you go, little buddy," I said. I tossed

some napkins in there, too. "And try not to spill the shake. That stuff is a bear to hose out."

I peeked down into my backpack and saw Floyd eat his entire burger in one bite. Then he started putting on a little play with Miss French Fry and the diabolical Mr. Straw.

"I'm glad he's got his backpack again," Sammy said after she sucked up about half her milk shake in one pull. "Also I have an ice cream headache. Ouch."

"Yeah, the fanny pack was kind of small, I guess. But it sure was good for speed. That little thing was super aerodynamic. I could have jumped over a building."

"You totally could have," Sammy agreed.

A half hour later we'd arrived at the edge of the Snood property on our bikes and found a big surprise.

"Wow, they've really beefed up security around here," I said.

Sammy scanned the property line in both directions. "They *must* be up to something."

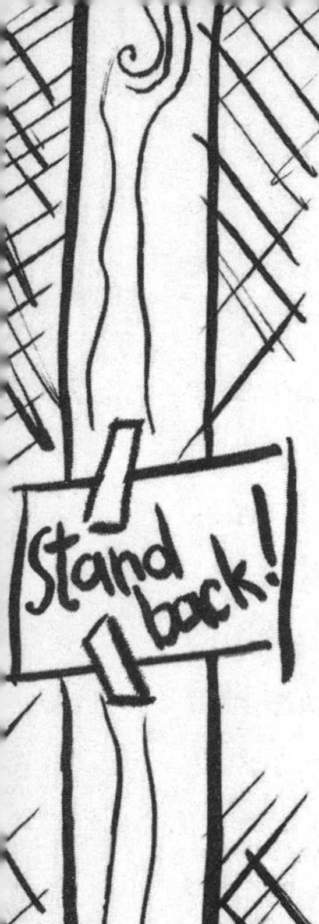
Stand back!

The Snoods had erected a twenty-foot-tall fence as far as we could see. It was made out of telephone poles and chicken wire.

"Check that out," I said, gazing up at the top of the nearest pole. A Styrofoam gargoyle was sitting there.

"It looks so real," Sammy whispered.

It did look real, partly because its head was slowly turning in our direction.

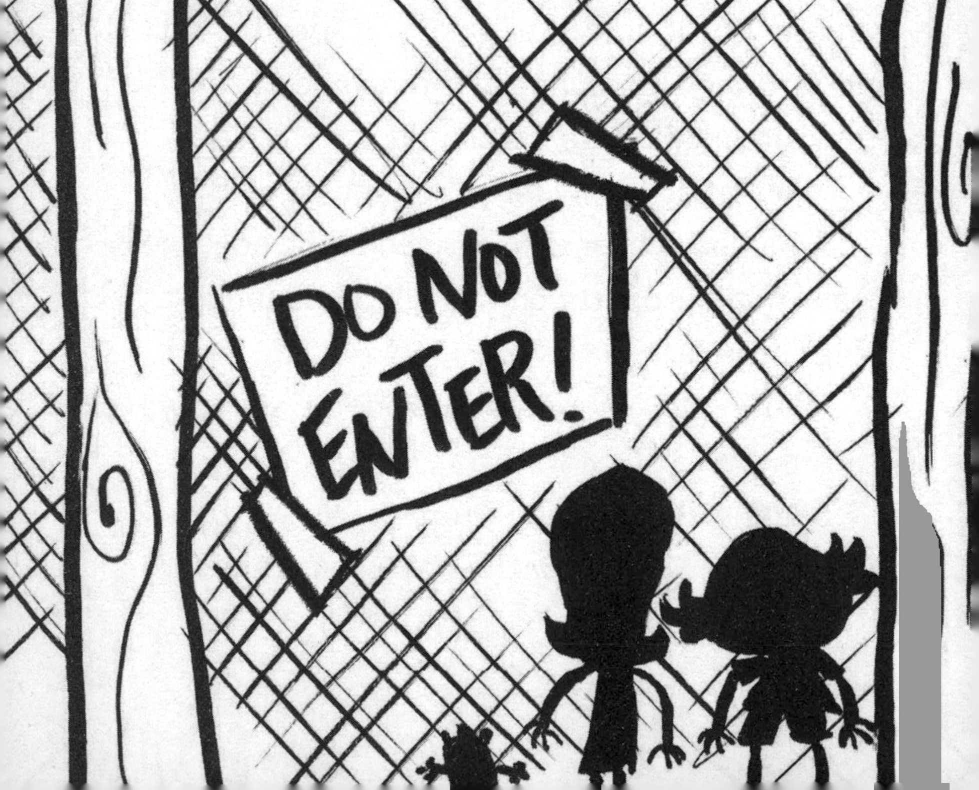
DO NOT ENTER!

"This is private Snood property," a voice boomed over our heads. "If you don't have an appointment, beat it!"

"This gargoyle has terrible manners," Sammy said.

"It must have a camera in its noggin. And speakers," I said.

There were signs printed on scraps of cardboard all along the fence line. They were stuck on there with silver duct tape. They said all kinds of stuff like:

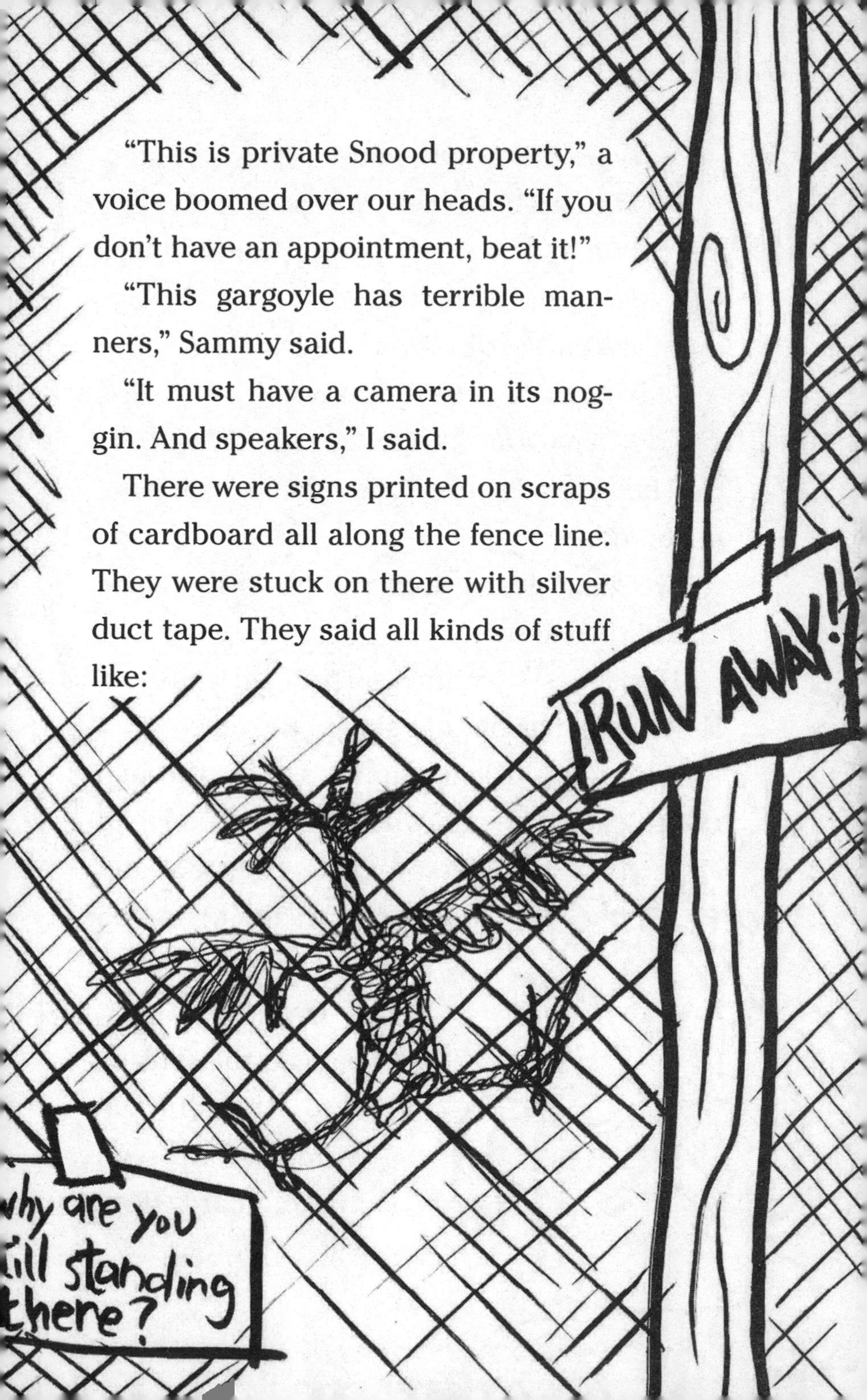
RUN AWAY!
why are you still standing there?

DO NOT ENTER!

STAND BACK!

RUN AWAY!

BE GONE WITH YOU!

WHY ARE YOU STILL STANDING THERE?

WE THINK YOU'RE DUMB.

BUY SNOODLES, BEST CANDY ON EARTH.

"The Snoods are odd ducks," Sammy observed.

Two giant guard dogs ran up to the fence and barked at us.

"Hey, guys!" Sammy said. "I missed you. How are things on that side of the fence?"

Both dogs licked Sammy's face through the chicken wire and whimpered. Then Floyd jumped out of my backpack and growled at them like an idiot. The dogs barked all over again and banged their heads into the chicken wire. We'd seen these guard dogs

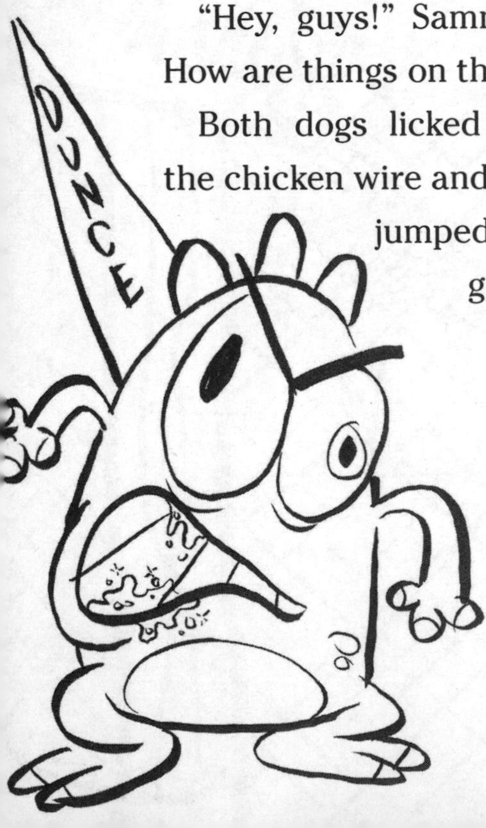
DUNCE

before (see my past journals!), but Sammy was so good with animals, it was like they weren't guard dogs at all. More like guard bunnies.

There was no way to go around the other side of the property because of a crazy thick sea of blackberry bushes on both sides of the road. Going too deep in there would be thorn city and we'd never make it out alive.

"How are we going to get inside?" Sammy said.

"I could jump over this fence with my bike," I said. "All we need to do is build a twenty-foot-tall ramp."

Sammy scratched the side of her head. "How long do you think it will take to build a ramp that big?"

That's one of the things I love about Sammy. Even if I come up with a harebrained idea, she doesn't say *that'll never work—it's harebrained!*

"I guess it would take maybe a month or so to build it," I admitted. "Scratch that idea."

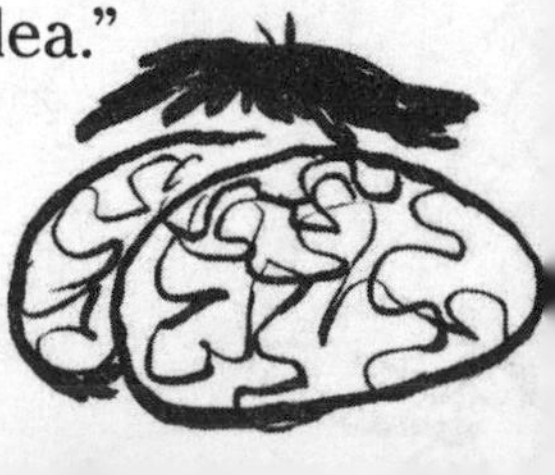

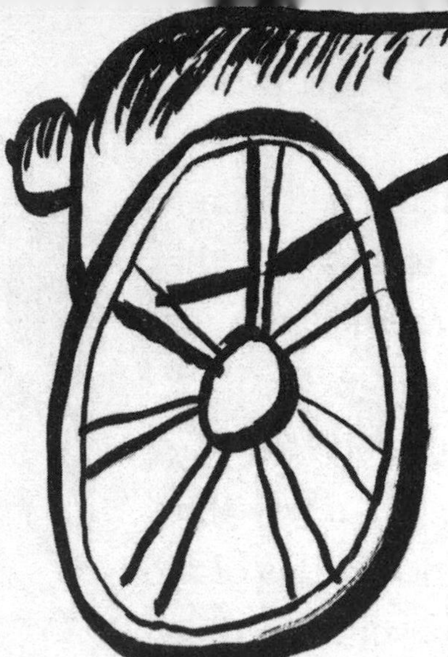

We racked our brains and came up with some other equally crazy ideas, like firing a cannonball at it or rolling over it with the biggest snowball in the world. Did I mention it's summer?

"Hey, where's Floyd?" Sammy asked after we'd been brainstorming harebrained ideas for a while.

I searched inside the backpack. "Bummer."

"He's not in there, is he?"

"Nope. And he spilled his milk shake all over our spy gear. The little stinker."

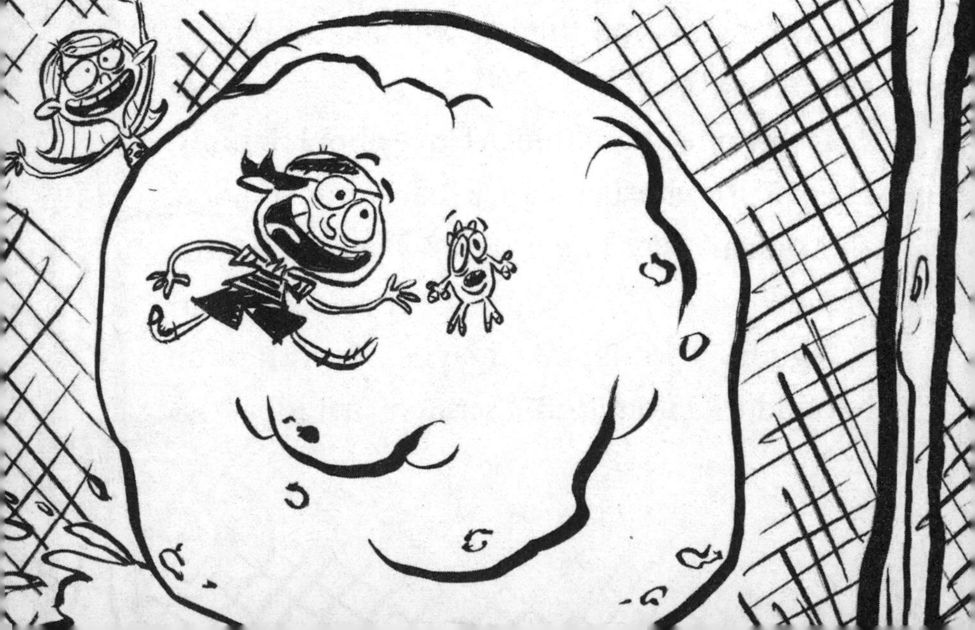

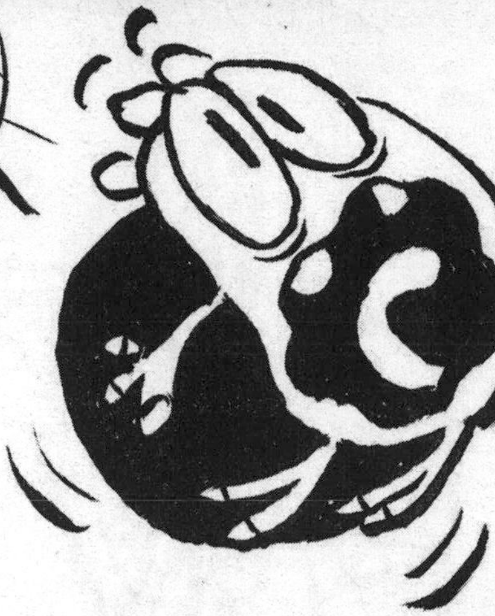

I pulled out a set of binoculars, Sammy's gag water pen, and a flashlight. They were all dripping with chocolate milk shake.

We went right up to the fence and leaned on it so the chicken wire bowed forward.

"I don't see him anywhere," Sammy said.

The Snood Candy Factory was way off in the distance behind the covered bridge and a line of trees. We were nowhere near figuring out how they were involved in the missing Fizzy Bottle Stuff and we'd lost Floyd. It was Snoods 2, Fuzzwonkers 0.

"What are those dogs looking at?" Sammy said. They were both sitting perfectly still, staring up into the sky.

"Must be a bird or a squirrel," I suggested.

Sammy and I both craned our necks up and up and up.

"What the?" I said. Floyd was sitting on the

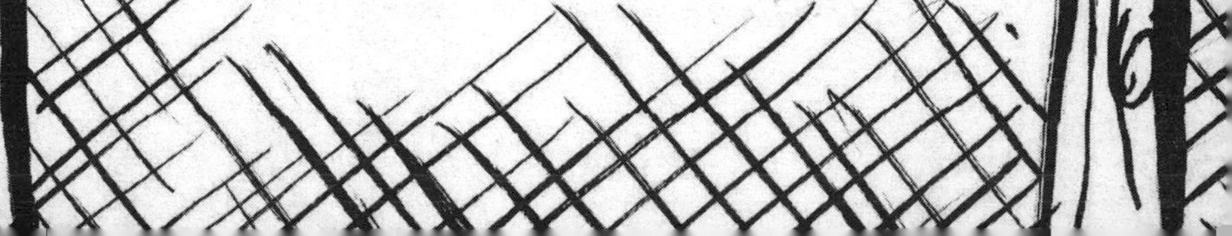

Styrofoam gargoyle head, talking into its ear. "What a knucklehead."

"He must have scaled it like Spider-Man!" Sammy said.

"If he can do it, so can we."

"Lead on, *el capitán*," Sammy said. "Let's scale this lame-wad fence!"

I threw all the yucked-up spy gear in my backpack and we marched to the blackberry bushes. They loomed up over us like a dark fog full of thorns.

"We'll need to cut through here so we can get to that fence pole," I said. The fence pole was about ten feet past the wall of blackberry bushes.

"Did you pack a machete?" Sammy asked. "Or a samurai sword? Or maybe a chain saw?"

I crouched down and peered into the gloom. "I keep asking my dad for better weapons, and he keeps saying no. I don't have any of that stuff. But I do have this."

I pulled out a pair of fingernail clippers.

"Perfect!" Sammy said. She took them from me and started clipping one of her nails. "So much better. I had a pinky nail I just had to clip. Now I can really concentrate."

She handed back the fingernail clippers and I put them in my pocket. Then I parted the sea of thorns and leaves and stepped inside. Once we were both in there, it felt like we'd entered a dark tunnel filled with sharp objects from head to toe.

"Ouch. Ouch. Ouch. Ouch. Ouch. Ouch. Ouch," I said. Sammy said the same thing. We

OUCH
OUCH
OUCH
OUCH
OUCH
OUCH
OUCH
OUCH
OUCH
OUCH
OUCH
OUCH
OUCH
OUCH
OUCH
OUCH
OUCH
OUCH OUCH
OUCH
OUCH
OUCH
OUCH
OUCH
OUCH
OUCH
OUCH
OUCH
OUCH
OUCH

both did, about a million times, until I hit my head on the fence pole and said, "Ouch," even louder.

"Now all we have to do is climb," Sammy said. "That should be the easy part."

I looked up at Floyd staring down at me. The little dork was lining up a wad of spit.

"Floyd!" I yelled. "Don't you dare drop a spit bomb!"

A little glob of fizzy spit headed my way.

"Retreat!" I yelled, backing up into Sammy. She said, "Ouch, ouch, ouch," and fell back on her butt. But at least Floyd's bomb missed me.

"Sorry about that," I said. "But it was life or death. You okay?"

"A-okay, palomino," Sammy said. "But I'd for sure like to get out of this thorny tangle of blackberry bush. It's the most uncomfortable place in the history of uncomfortable places."

I moved back to the pole and stared up at Floyd. "If you do that again I won't help you train for Fizzies vs. Food anymore. You'll be on your own."

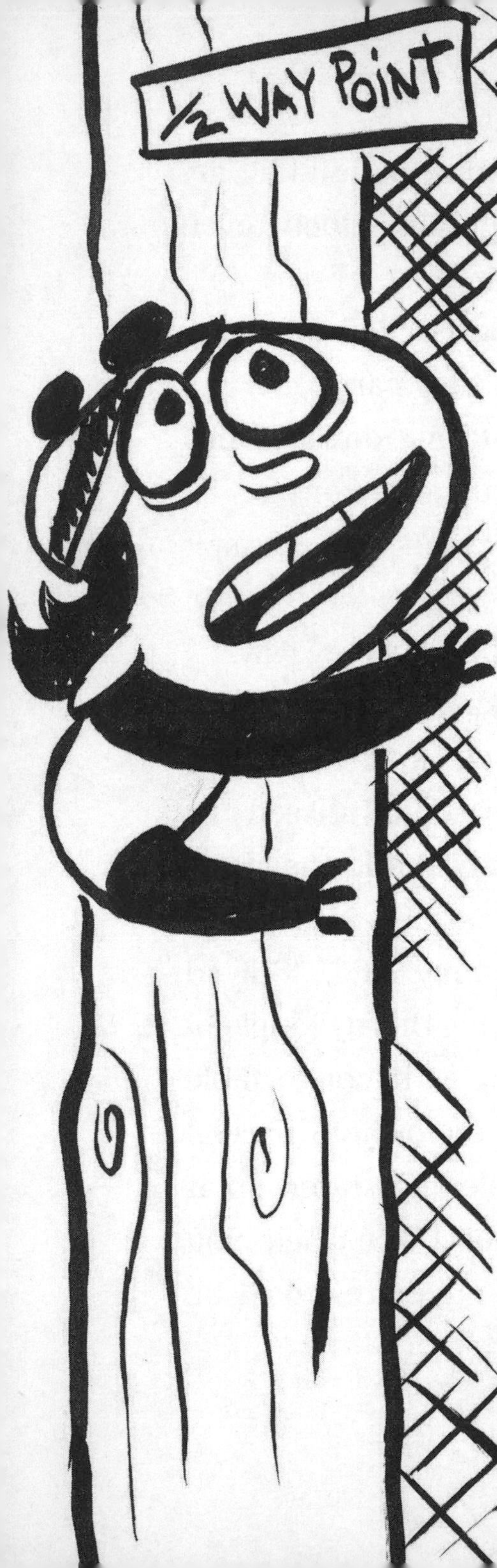
1/2 WAY POINT

Floyd crossed his arms over his chest like I'd ruined his whole week, but he stopped dropping spit bombs on me.

I scaled the fence by sticking my fingers and shoes into the chicken wire and hugging the pole like a panda bear. It didn't take long to reach the halfway point.

"You're like a monkey!" Sammy said. "I'm heading up."

If I slipped and fell I'd land right on Sammy's head, so I was extra careful with every move. I heard a noise at the top of the pole and glanced up. Floyd had ripped one of the Styrofoam arms off the gargoyle and he was holding it out over my head.

"Don't even think about it, bub," I said, as if that was going to stop him.

He dropped the arm and it bonked me right in the noggin, then bounced into the blackberry bushes below. It looked like a severed zombie arm.

"Floyd!" I yelled. He was already busy trying to tear the gargoyle's head off, but he was having trouble with it. I cut the distance between us to a few feet before the gargoyle head popped off. There were a lot of wires hanging out of the severed head, where the camera leads were stored. Floyd chewed through them right about the time I showed up at the top of the pole.

I narrowed my eyes.

Floyd stopped chewing and let the gargoyle head fall out of his paws. It hung upside down against its chest. Floyd had a really sad look on his face.

"It's okay, little buddy," I said. "And, hey,

you disabled this camera so they can't see us up here. Good job!"

Floyd perked up as Sammy's head bonked into the bottom of my foot, so I climbed over the top and started down the other side.

A few minutes later we were on the ground inside the Snood property line.

Now all we had to do was figure out what they were up to!

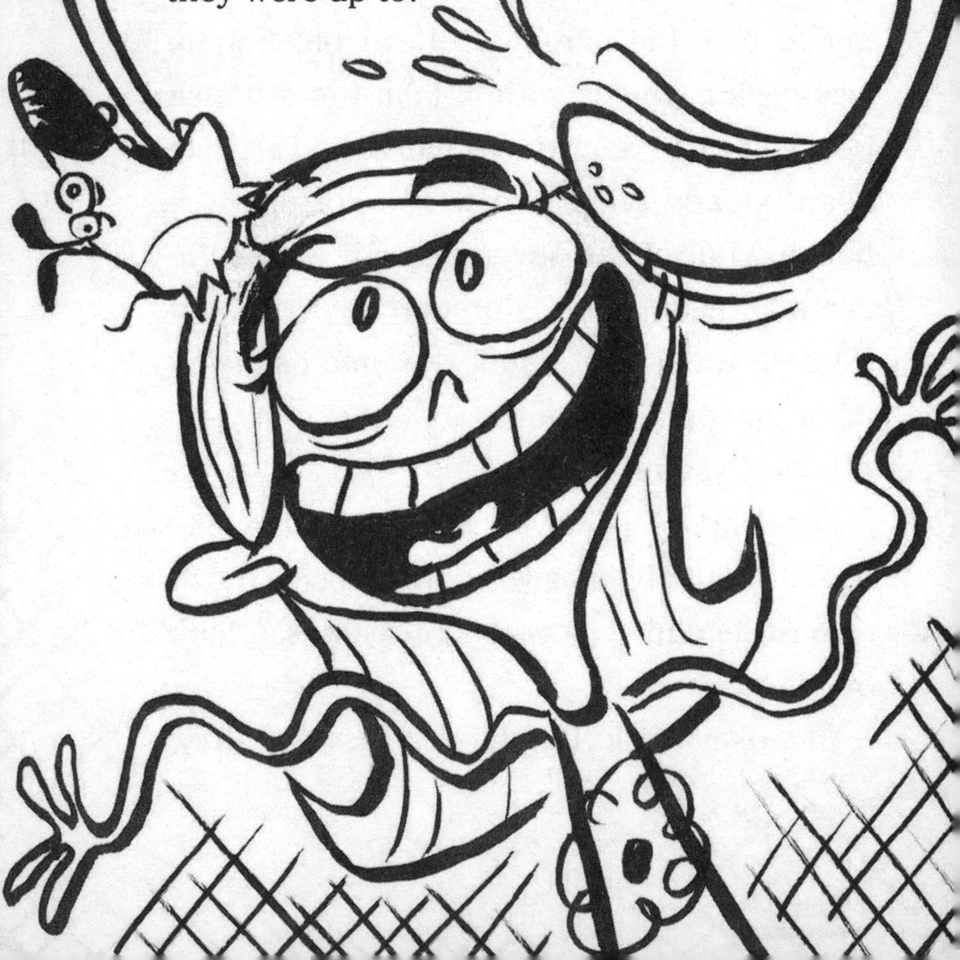

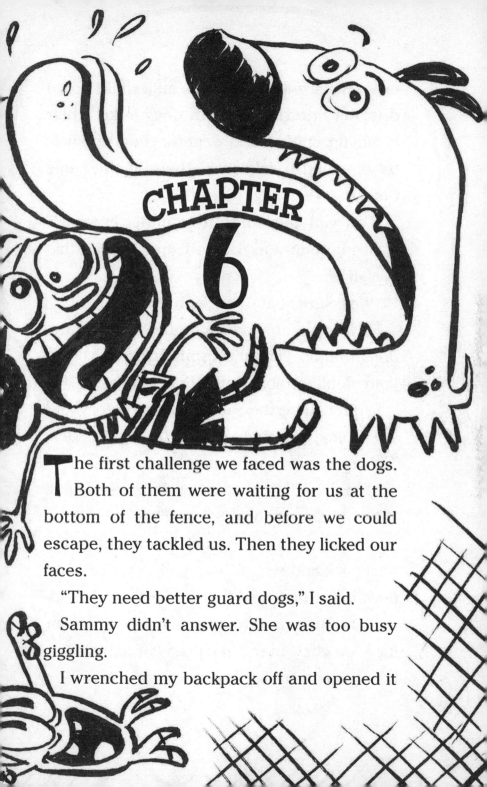

CHAPTER 6

The first challenge we faced was the dogs. Both of them were waiting for us at the bottom of the fence, and before we could escape, they tackled us. Then they licked our faces.

"They need better guard dogs," I said.

Sammy didn't answer. She was too busy giggling.

I wrenched my backpack off and opened it

up so the scent of chocolate milk shake could drift out into the air. Both dogs jerked their heads up, sniffed, and went for the bag. Their heads could barely fit in there at the same time.

"Can you keep these two under control?" I asked Sammy as I stood up and brushed myself off.

"Well, sure I can. They're my pals!"

Floyd sat on my shoulder and yelled at the dogs to stop vandalizing his backpack. "Get your slobbery noses out of my house!"

I stared up at the Snood Candy Factory and saw steam pouring out of the smokestack. There was also a lot of noise in there.

"They're at full production for sure," I said. "The building is shaking."

The dogs got their giant heads out of my backpack and stood there panting. The good news was when I reached in to get my spy binoculars, they were totally cleaned off. Except for a few chew marks the dogs left behind, the binoculars were in perfect working order.

"Come on, you guys," I said. "Let's go around back and see if there's anything suspicious."

We crept along the fence line and I handed the binoculars to Sammy.

"Wow, the Snood Candy Factory is a long way off. We should have brought more snacks," Sammy said.

She was looking through the wrong end of the binoculars, so I turned them around for her. She pointed them at my head so I could see her gigantic eyeballs.

"I don't think we're going to find anything out here," I said. "And it's really tough getting inside."

"How about we try the roof?" Sammy said. "If we can scale that humongous fence, the Snood Candy Factory will be no problemo."

"And, hey, look," I said as we came around the back side of the factory. "There's even a ladder stuck to the side of the building. It's like we're *supposed* to climb up there."

Floyd jumped off my shoulder and landed on one of the rungs. He sniffed it, licked it, and tried to eat it. Then he turned and nodded like it was okay to proceed.

We went up the side of the building in no time flat, but the dogs wouldn't stop barking from down below.

"Aw, they miss me," Sammy said once we got to the top and looked back down. "It's okay, guys. I'll be right back."

She picked up an old shoe that someone had left on the roof and threw it as far as she could. Sammy was a very good thrower, so it sailed clean over the chicken wire fence.

Down below, the back door to the Snood Candy Factory opened and Mr. Snood came out, holding something that looked like a flamethrower.

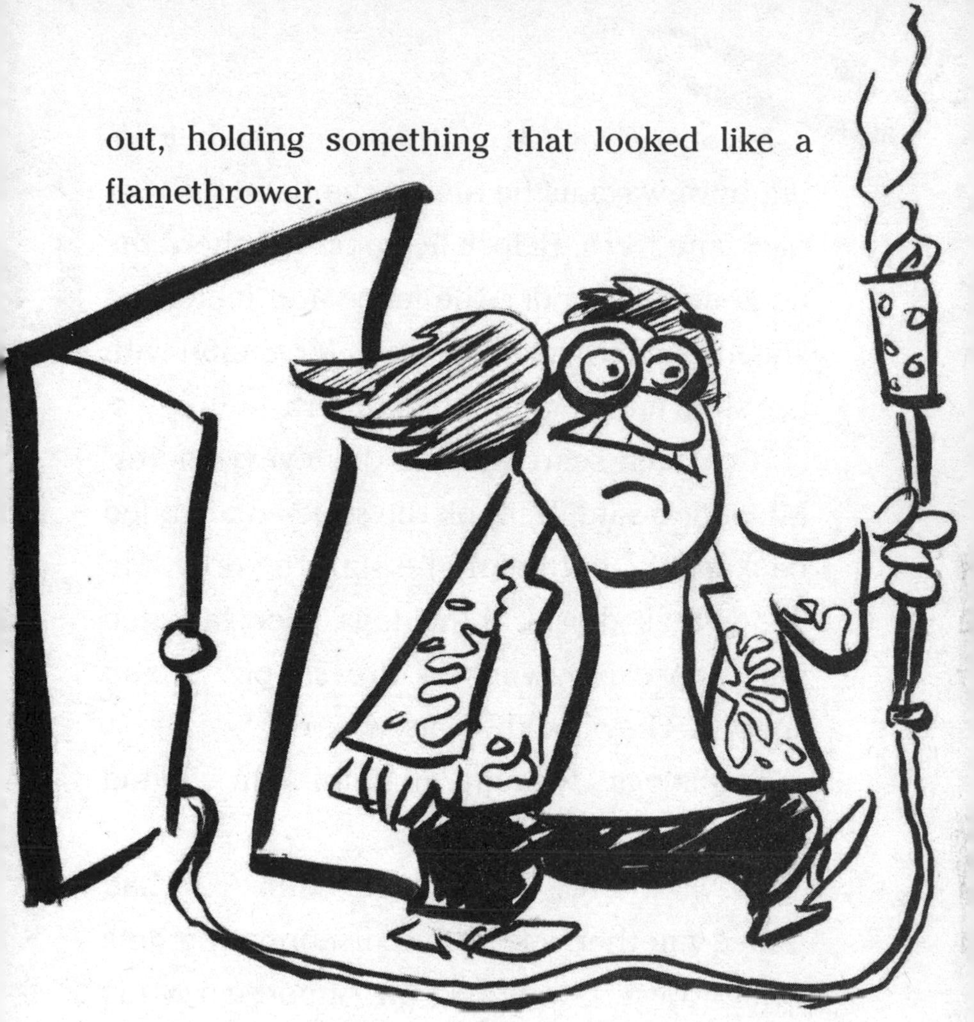

"Whoa," I said. "He's serious about security."

He looked around the back of the building and yelled at the dogs to stop barking so much. They were over at the fence, trying to dig underneath and get the shoe.

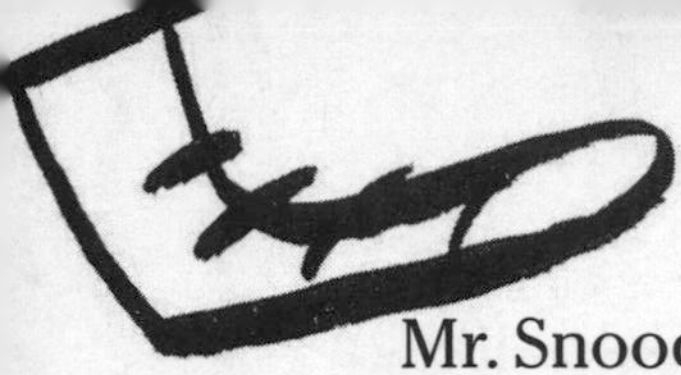

Mr. Snood walked out there cautiously, looking both ways as he aimed the flamethrower back and forth. Before he could get there the dogs made it under the fence and found the shoe. One of them came up to Mr. Snood with the shoe hanging out of its mouth.

"I've been searching for this everywhere!" Mr. Snood said. He took the shoe and headed back inside, but before he shut the door, Mr. Snood looked back at the dogs. "Keep a watch out. Those Fuzzwonkers are snoopy snoop snoops. They could be anywhere!"

The dogs whimpered and Mr. Snood slammed the door shut.

"Hey, where's Floyd?" I said. He had pulled another one of his disappearing acts while we were watching Mr. Snood carry his flamethrower around. Sammy searched the grounds with the binoculars.

"I don't see him anywhere out there. He must be up here somewhere."

There was so much action in the factory

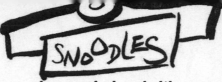

down below, the roof shook like we were in the middle of an earthquake. We dodged all kinds of old parts and big metal boxes and the bottom of the smokestack. Floyd was plastered to a skylight like he'd done a belly flop from a high dive. He was lying there, staring into the factory.

"Hey, best good buddy," I said. "Can you see anything down there?"

Floyd didn't answer, so we stuck our faces against the glass, too.

The factory was in full-tilt, no-holds-barred, out-of-control production. The conveyor belts hummed in every direction, carrying boxes and boxes marked SNOODLES. Over to our left was a ginormous vat full of something that was frothing, fizzing, and boiling.

"Well, it's official," Sammy said as she peeled her eyeballs off the glass and looked at me. "They're using Fuzzwonker Fizz down there."

A slew of robotic arms were grabbing Fuzz-wonker Fizz bottles from boxes, uncapping

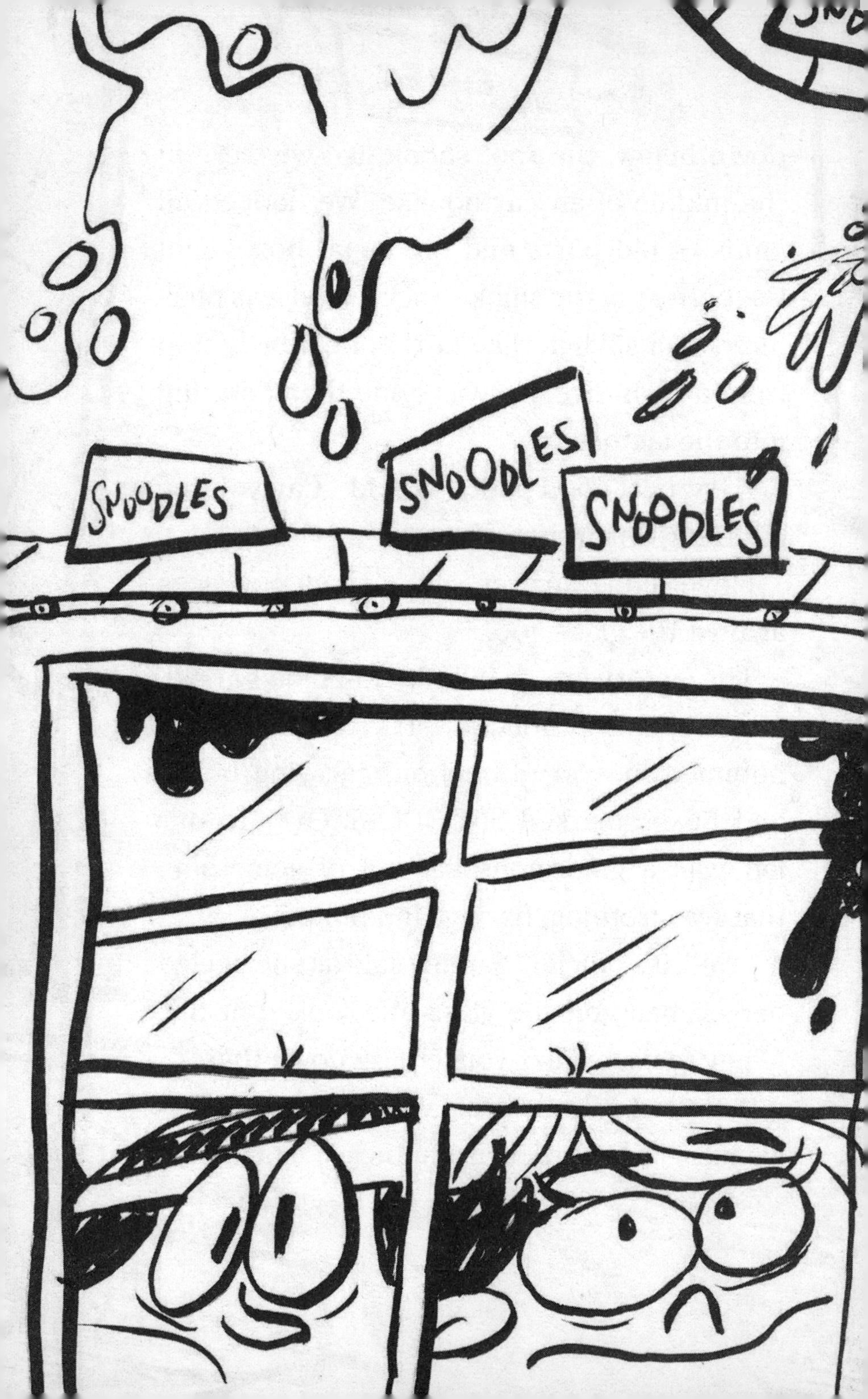
SNOODLES
SNOODLES
SNOODLES

them, and pouring the contents into the vat.

"They're dumping all our Fuzzwonker Fizz in there!" I yelled.

The Fuzzwonker Fizz was being pumped through a tube into another vat and then another, where more ingredients were being added, and then something that looked like taffy was being stored in metal garbage cans.

"It's packages and packages of Snoodles!" I said. "This is outrageous."

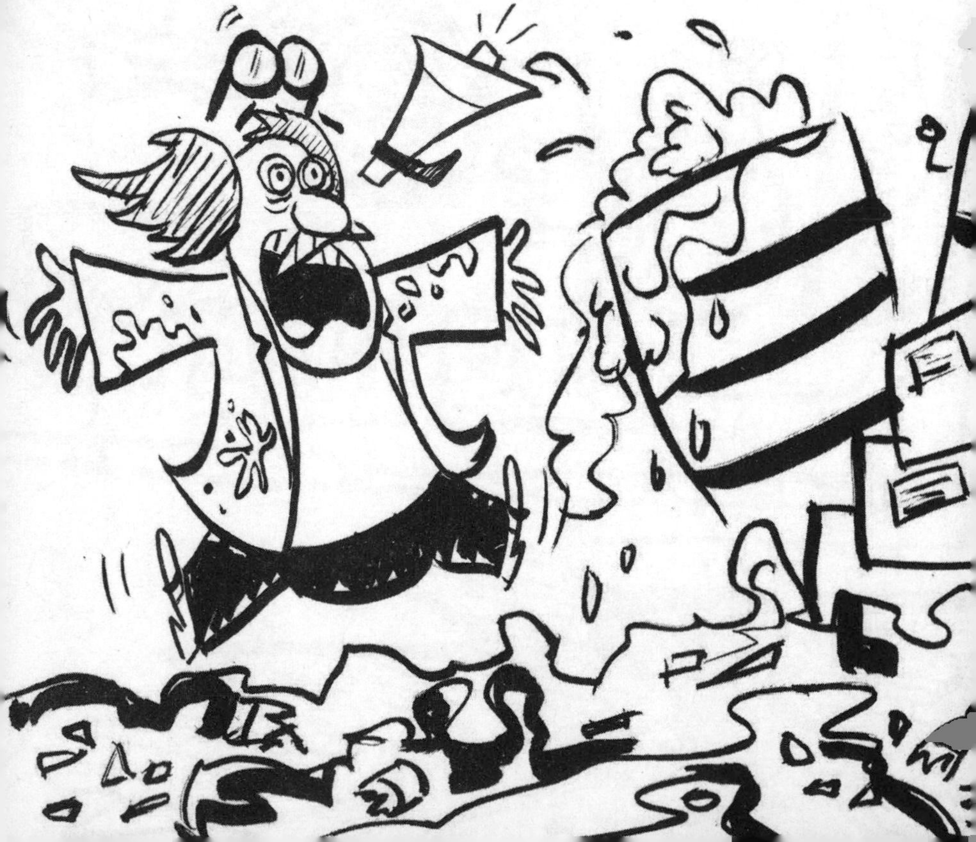

Garvin Snood was down there driving a forklift and bumping into stuff. He was a terrible driver and his dad kept yelling at him to be careful. Garvin picked up a giant box on a pallet that was filled with empty Fuzzwonker Fizz bottles and headed down a ramp that led underground toward the side of the building.

Mr. Snood yelled through a megaphone. We could barely hear him from outside the skylight, but I was sure he'd mentioned a red barn.

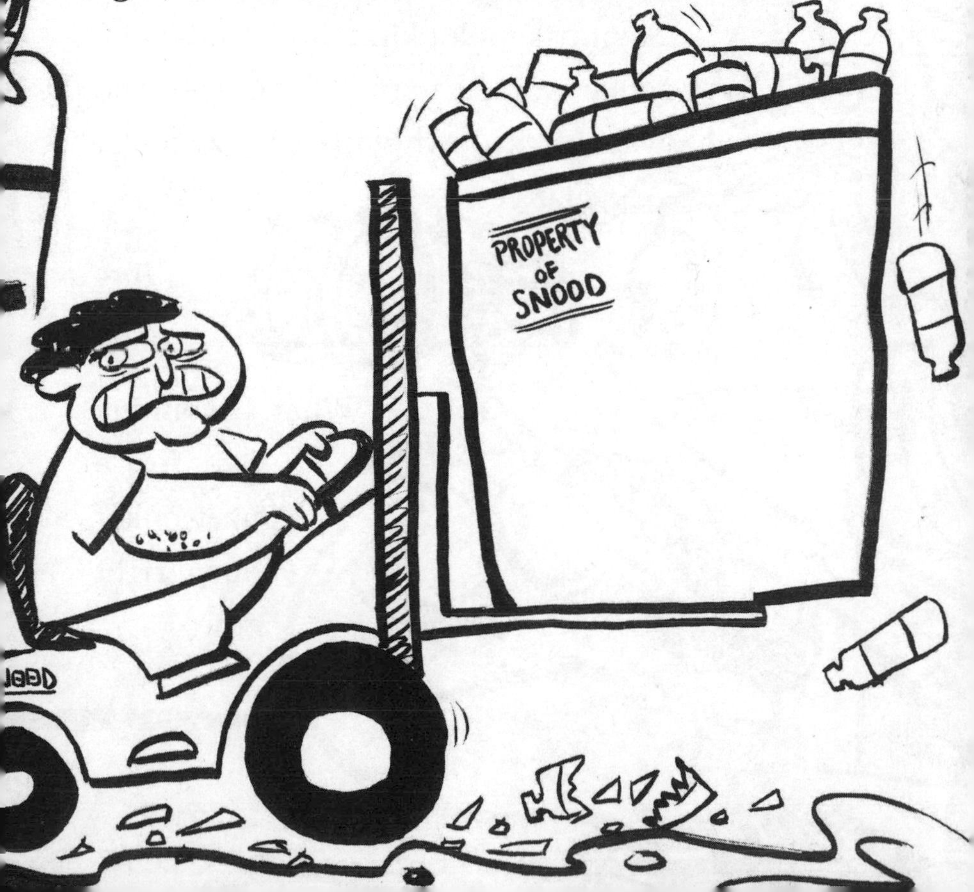
PROPERTY
OF
SNOOD

"They must be storing all our bottles at some red barn on the property," I said.

"Follow me," Sammy said. She bolted for the edge of the roof and stared into the binoculars again.

After about ten seconds a wooden door blew open from the ground and the forklift drove out onto the Snoods' property.

"Where do you think he's taking our bottles?" I asked.

Sammy kept looking through the binoculars. "He's eating Snoodles. And washing it down with a Fuzzwonker Fizz."

"What I wouldn't give for a Fuzzwonker burp right now.

What a big jerk."

That side of the Snood property went on forever. It turned into a forest, and once Garvin and his dumb forklift got far enough away, they disappeared down a pathway into the trees.

We had to know where Garvin was taking all our Fuzzwonker Fizz bottles.

"Let's go, guys," I said. "It's time for Operation Chase-Garvin-Snood-into-the-Woods."

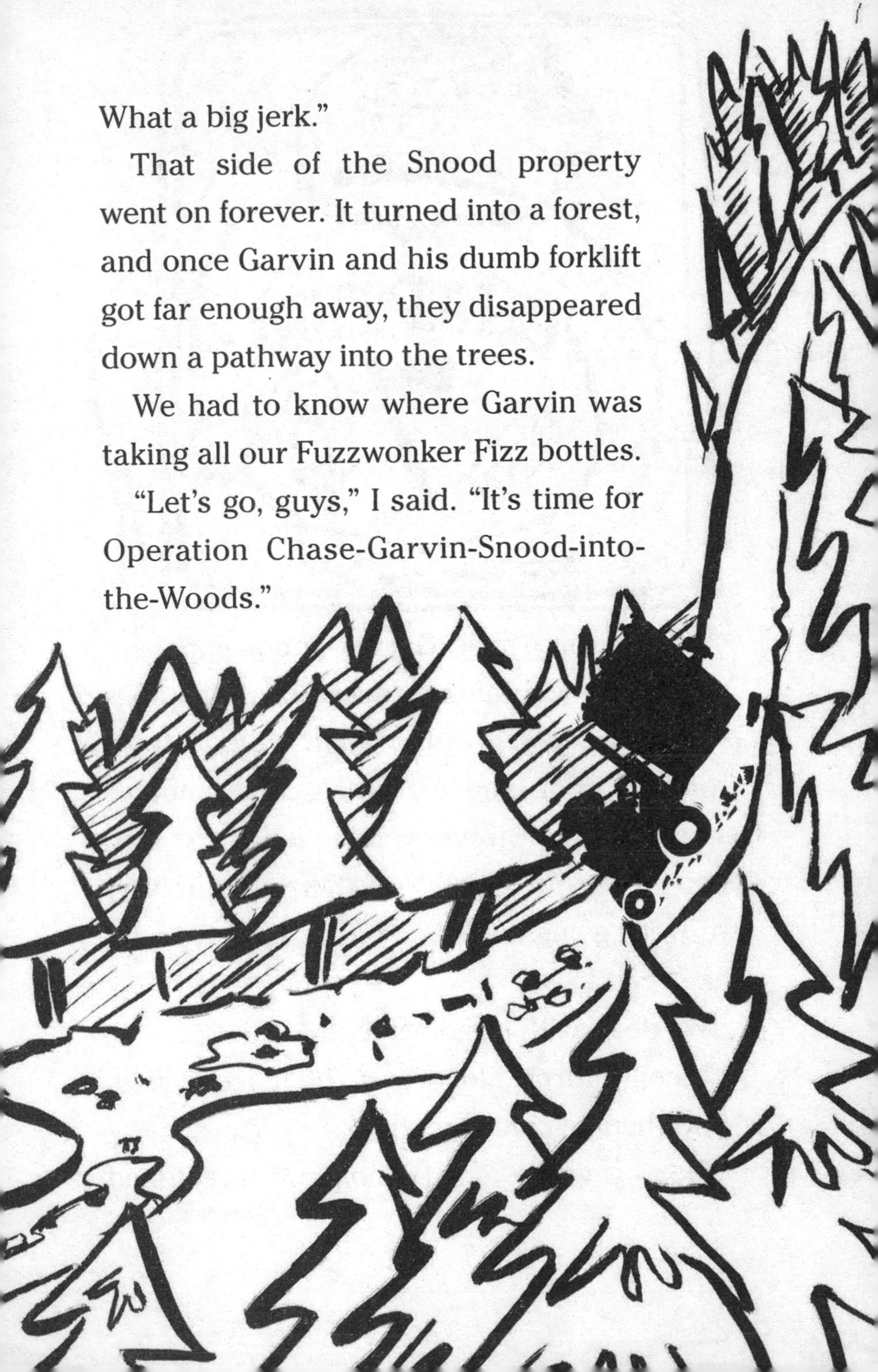

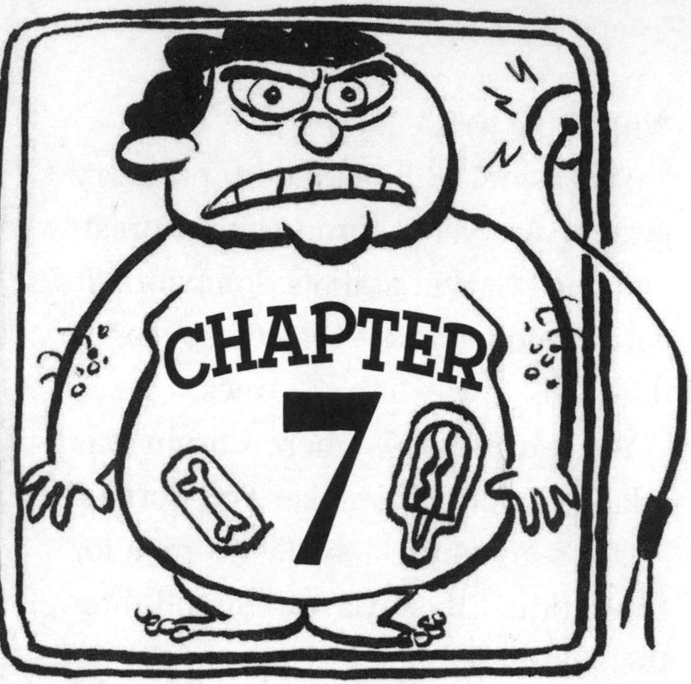
CHAPTER
7

Operation Chase-Garvin-Snood-into-the-Woods got off to a rocky start. The dogs were in a mood to play when we got down from the roof, and we didn't have another shoe we could throw over the fence. We also didn't have our bikes, and there was no way we were going after Garvin on foot. It could take years!

We dealt with the dogs first.

"I could throw Floyd over the fence," I said. "And then he could run back."

Floyd gave me a dirty look and threatened

to lick my face off, so we kept thinking.

"How about this rock?" Sammy said. She picked up a rock about the size of a watermelon and tossed it as hard as she could. It almost hit her in the foot. "Okay, forget about the rock."

The dogs kept staring at us, and then one of them barked. Then the other one barked.

"We can't have these two nitwits chasing us through the forest," I said. "And if they keep barking, Mr. Snood will come back out here with his flamethrower and blowtorch our butts off."

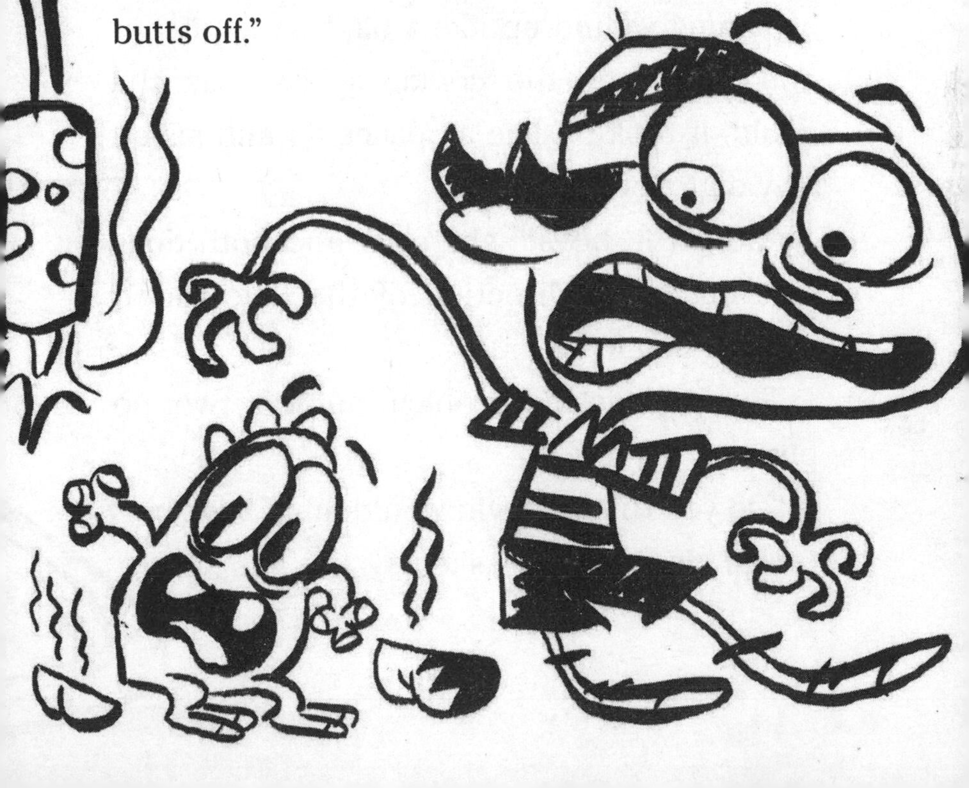

Floyd talked into my ear.

"Why didn't you say that before?" I answered, then I pulled off my backpack and opened it up. Inside, I unzipped a small compartment. I found a chocolate chip cookie that was harder than granite. I banged it against a metal pipe attached to the Snood Candy Factory and it clanged.

"I was saving it for a special occasion," Floyd said.

I handed the petrified cookie to Sammy. "It doesn't get any specialer than this."

Sammy wound up like a big-league pitcher and sidearmed the cookie as hard as she could. It took off like a spaceship and sailed way out over the fence.

"Go get it, boys!" she said, and both dogs tore off in the direction of the hole they'd already dug to get out.

Then we tackled problem number two: no bikes.

"Do you think Garvin would mind if we borrowed his?" Sammy asked.

As long as we didn't take Garvin's bike off the Snood property, I didn't see why he would mind if we rode it around for a while. There was only one problem: Garvin's bike was HUGE. Even for Garvin Snood, who was bigger than we were, it was enormous. We found it leaned up against the Snood Candy Factory.

"How are we going to ride *that* thing?" I asked.

Sammy furrowed her brow and stared at the bike. Then she had an aha moment.

"Could we each work one pedal and half the handlebars?"

It sounded completely impossible and totally weird. So of course I loved the idea.

I grabbed the bike and wobbled it in between us. Dang, that bike was big! The top of the wheels were about as high as my armpits. Floyd jumped up and down on my shoulder like we were about to get on a roller coaster and do some serious loop-de-loops. Sammy put one foot on the pedal on her side and held the handlebar with one hand. I put my foot

81

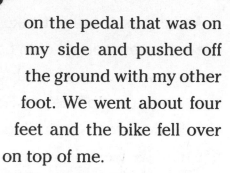

on the pedal that was on my side and pushed off the ground with my other foot. We went about four feet and the bike fell over on top of me.

"This is going to be harder than I thought," I said.

"Come on, newbie," Sammy said. "We can do this."

So we tried again. Actually we tried nine more times. We bashed into the Snood Candy Factory twice, the bike fell on one or the other of us six times, and we flipped over the handlebars once. It was the most fun I've had in weeks.

On the tenth try we started getting the hang of it. Sammy would push down on her pedal and I'd drift up into the air. Then I'd push down on my pedal and she would rise up. It felt kind of like being on a teeter-totter.

"Hey," I said. "We're doing it!"

We took off down the pathway into the woods and bounced off a couple of trees. Then we hit a boulder and flipped over the handlebars.

"This is a blast!" Sammy said. "Let's do it again."

By the time we'd crashed another six or seven times, we totally had it down cold. We

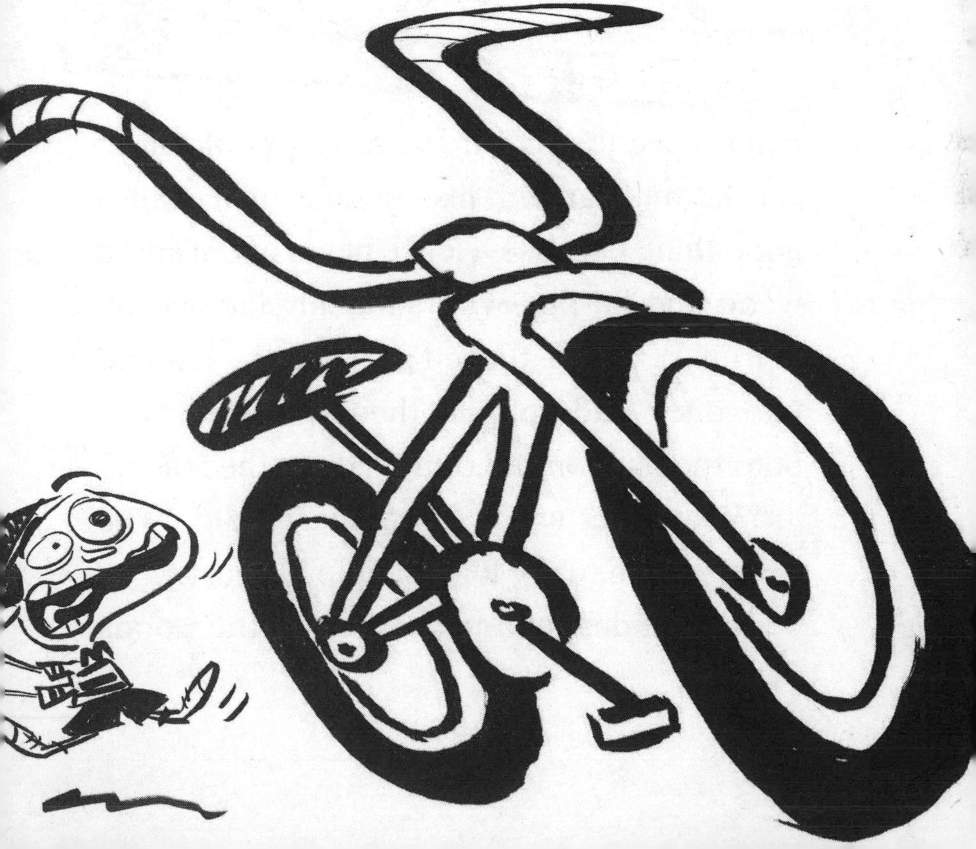

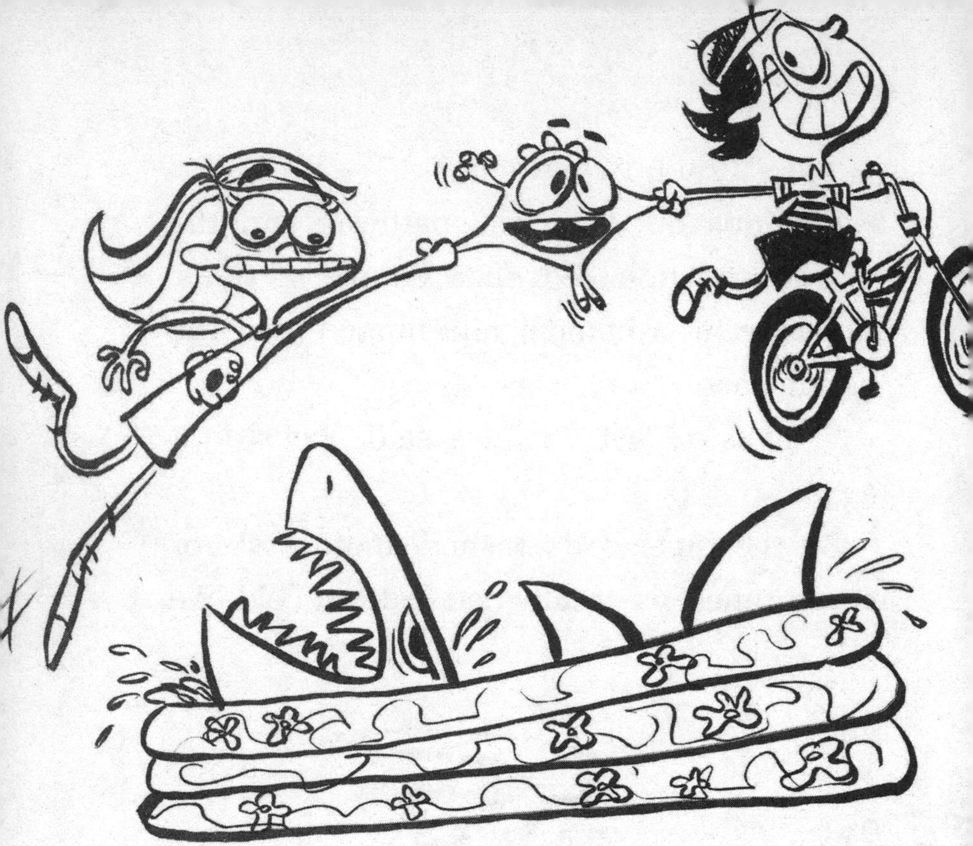

could have jumped a swimming pool full of sharks and landed like pros, which was a good thing because a fence made out of scrap wood and barbed wire suddenly loomed up in front of us. We turned sharp to the left and into thick underbrush, then careened back onto the path on the other side of the fence.

"Whew, that was a close one," I said. "The Snoods have really loaded up on security."

We went deeper and deeper into the woods

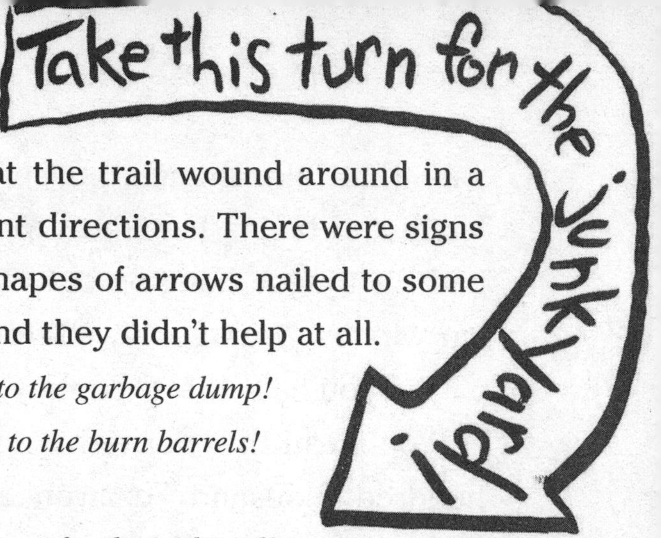
Take this turn for the junkyard!

and found that the trail wound around in a million different directions. There were signs made in the shapes of arrows nailed to some of the trees, and they didn't help at all.

This way to the garbage dump!

Thataway to the burn barrels!

Swamp!

Take this turn for the junkyard!

Red barn, over here!

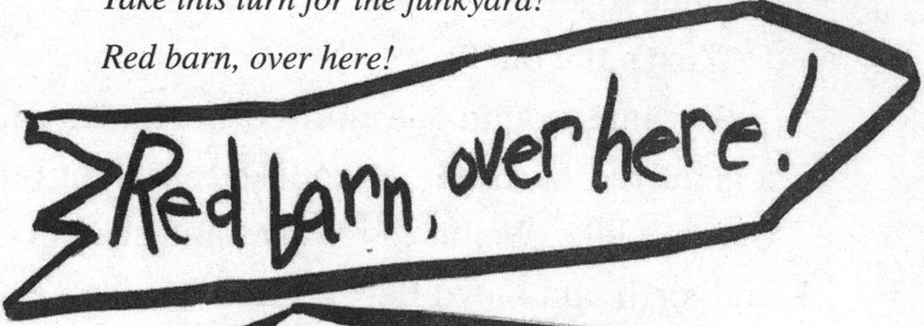
Red barn, over here!

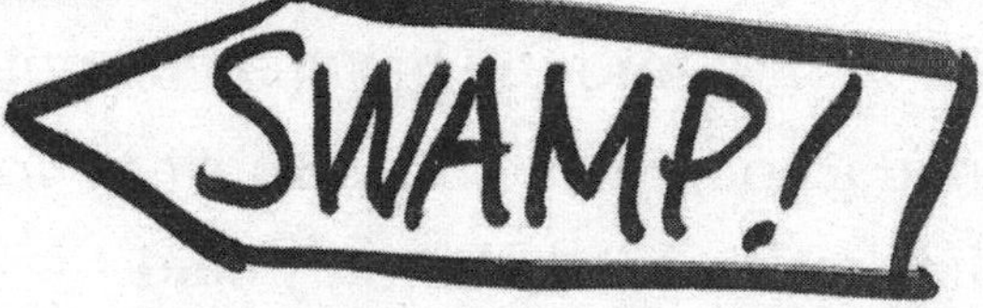
SWAMP!

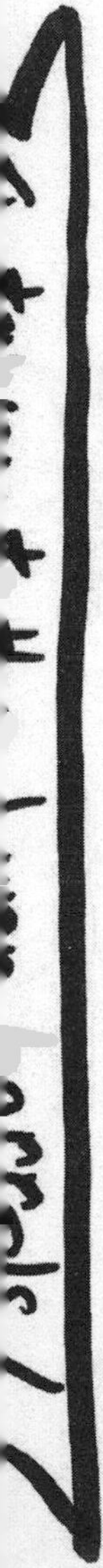

We followed the signs to the red barn and figured whatever Garvin was doing it was the most secret thing in the crummy Snoods' universe. The woods got darker and the path got narrower and curvier. Floyd shivered, because he's kind of a chicken when it comes to dark woods. We were like NASCAR drivers

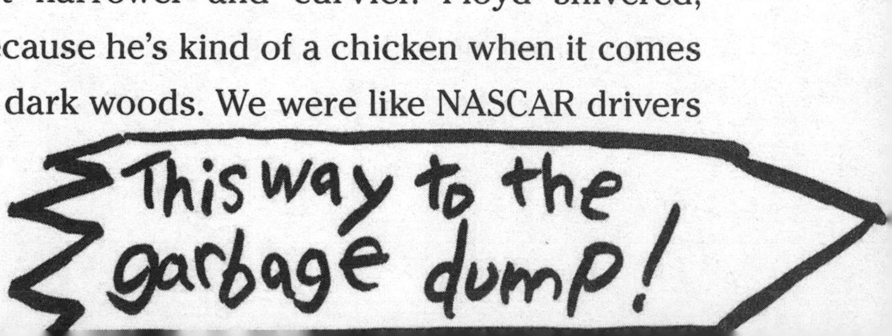
This way to the garbage dump!

with that bike though, cutting corners perfectly and taking her up to top speed. Floyd had his tongue hanging out like a dog out a car window. We were a well-oiled machine!

"Did you hear that?" Sammy asked.

"You mean that noise that sounds like one hundred thousand Fuzzwonker Fizz bottles banging together?" I asked.

"That's the one!"

We came around one more corner and BAM, a giant red barn nearly knocked us right off Garvin's bike. We hit the brakes and slid back and forth and Floyd flew off my shoulder. He went face-first into the barn, but Sammy and I stopped a couple of inches short of crashing.

"Man, we're good," Sammy said.

"You okay, buddy?" I asked Floyd.

He slid down the side of the barn like a glob of waffle batter and stood up. When he turned around he had a dazed, happy look on his face.

"Best. Ride. Ever," he said.

"I know, right?" I agreed.

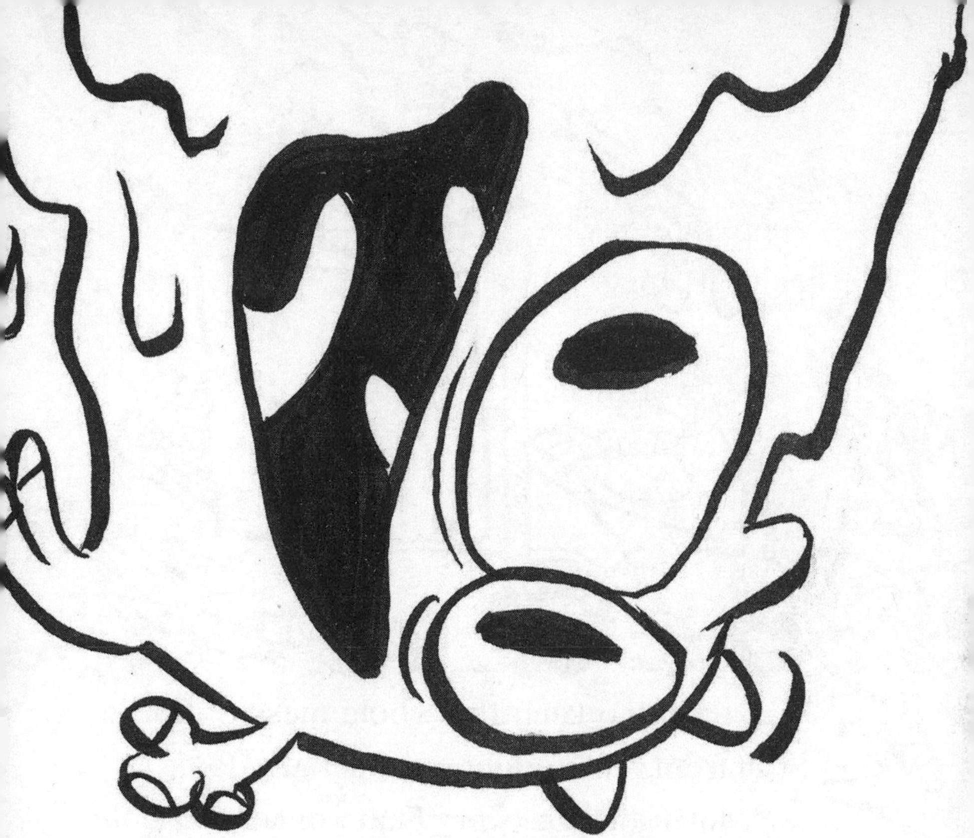

Inside we could hear the sound of a machine doing some kind of villainous work. We tiptoed to the barn door and it creaked when we opened it. We peeked inside.

“It’s a good thing Fuzzwonker Bottle Stuff is incredibly strong,” Sammy whispered.

And boy was she right. Garvin was in there using the forklift to move piles and piles of bottles into bigger piles and piles of bottles. He’d already dumped the box of new ones and

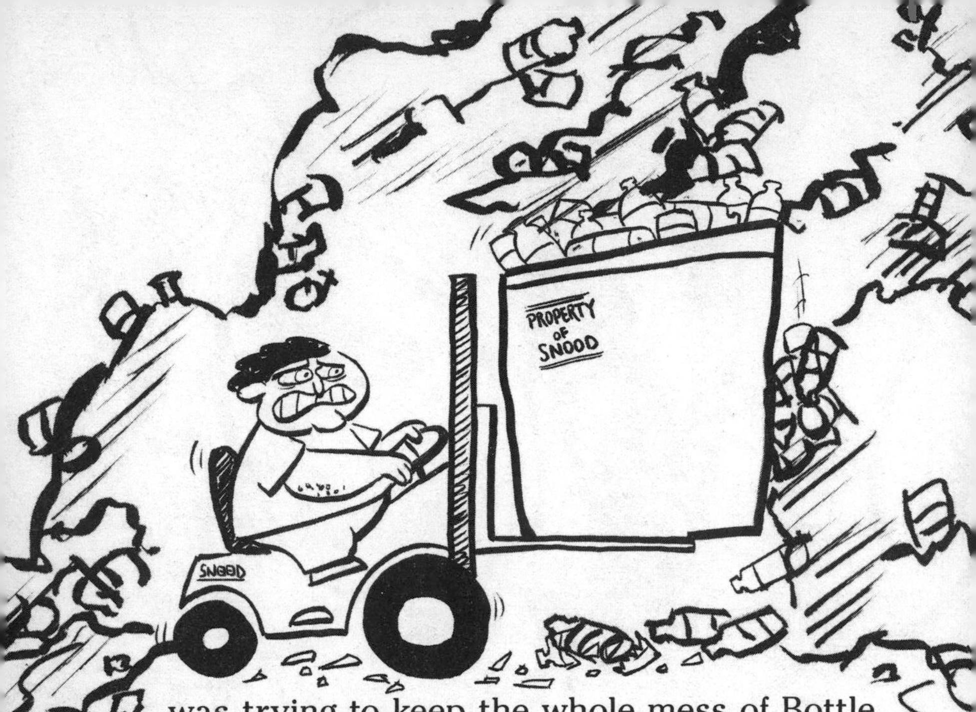
PROPERTY OF SNOOD
SNOOD

was trying to keep the whole mess of Bottle Stuff from rolling right out the barn door.

"That's gotta be every Fuzzwonker Fizz bottle in the world," I said.

Now we had all the evidence we needed. But what were we going to do? Floyd jumped into the backpack and milled around in there. Then he showed up on my shoulder and pulled my earlobe very close. He had the gag water pen in his paw, and he squirted it all over the side of my face. Then Floyd drew a map of the Snood property on his belly. The map included the location of the barn with some

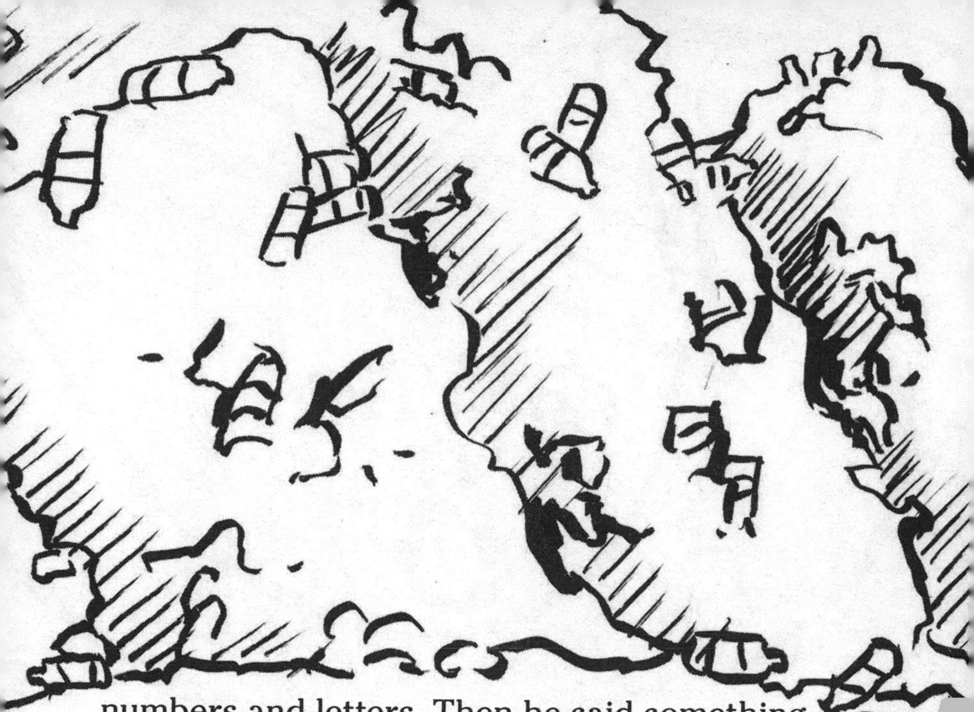

numbers and letters. Then he said something that made me smile like a baby eating birthday cake.

I turned to Sammy. "Floyd has an idea that's almost for sure impossible to pull off."

Sammy went over and got on her side of the bike with a look of total determination on her face.

"What are we waiting for?" Sammy said. "Let's do it!"

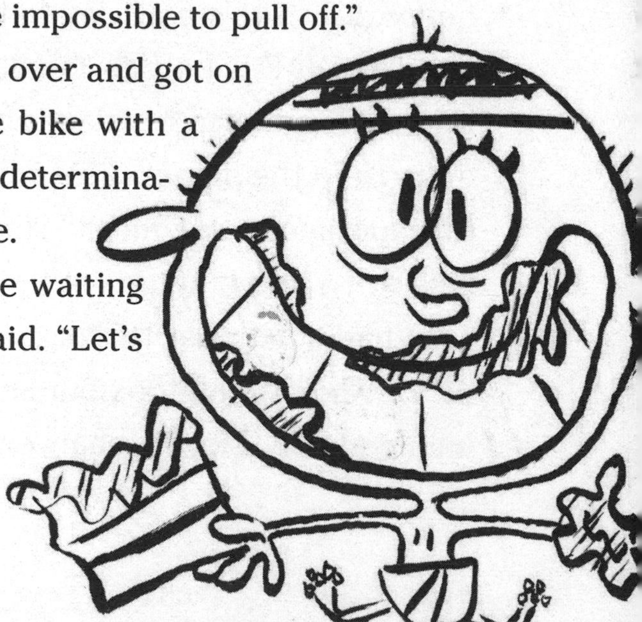

CHAPTER 8

It took quite a while to ride Garvin's colossal bike back to the Snood Candy Factory, scale the fence, and take our own bikes back to my house. It had taken all day to track down the Fuzzwonker Fizz bottles, but at least we made it home for dinner. My dad is a food-mad scientist, and the dinner table is where he tends to experiment the most. This is especially true when he's bummed out.

"What's for dinner, Dr. Fuzzwonker?" Sammy asked while we all took our seats around the kitchen table. Floyd's chair sat up very high

so he was right up next to his plate.

My dad had his mondo chef's hat on. It nearly touched the ceiling. He loved explaining what he'd made for dinner almost as much as he loved making it.

"I'm glad you asked, Sammy," Dr. Fuzzwonker said. Then he began pointing out all the unusual stuff on the table. "This is a dish I like to call the Lasagna Shooter."

There was a long tube sitting on every plate. They were made of clear plastic and they were about two feet long. I picked mine up.

"There's one full serving of lasagna in each Lasagna Shooter," my dad said. "And you can shoot lasagna a total of six times for each tube. Like this."

Dr. Fuzzwonker picked up the Lasagna Shooter on his plate, aimed it at Floyd, and tapped one of the six buttons along the top of the tube. The Lasagna Shooter bucked like a shotgun and one mouthful of lasagna shot out the end. Floyd had his mouth open like a fishbowl, and the lasagna slapped against his tongue. He started chewing happily.

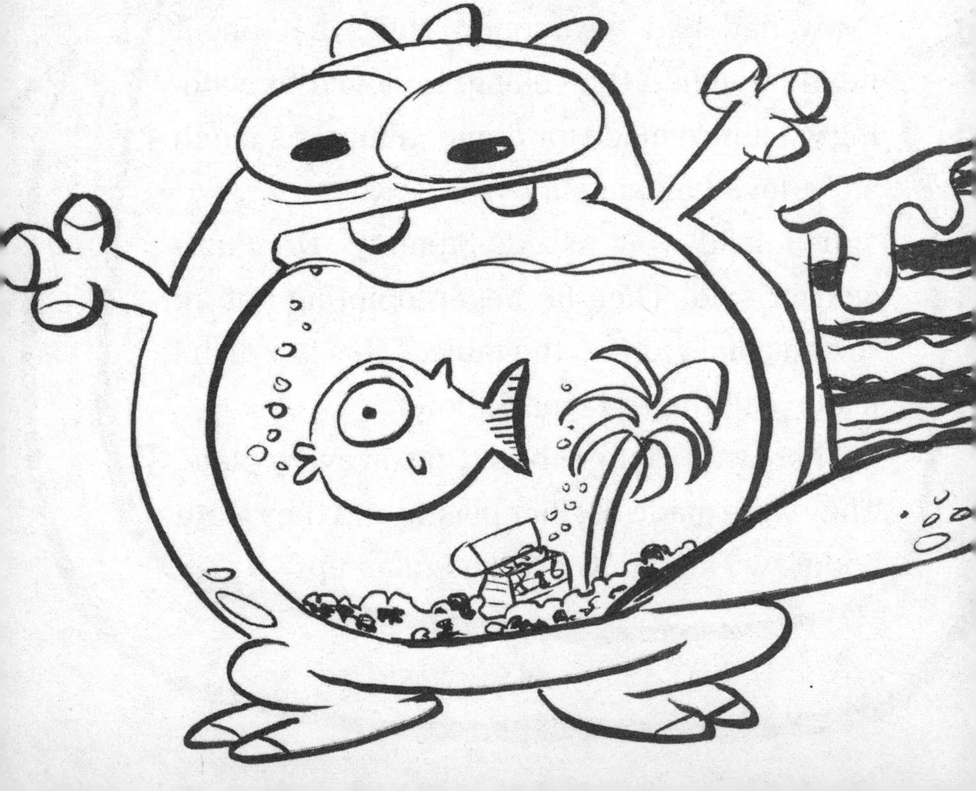

"I love Lasagna Shooters!" Sammy said. She pointed hers at me and fired before I could turn around and a glob of lasagna hit me in the side of the head. After that we got the hang of it, and I shot my dad twice and Sammy once and had no problem hitting them right in the kisser. When I looked over at Floyd, he was trying to turn his Lasagna Shooter around and fire it into his own mouth.

"Incoming, Floyd!" I yelled, and then all three of us shot my best good buddy at the same time. He caught them all and then turned his Lasagna Shooter on us.

"This is way too much fun," I said while I munched. "Great job, Dad. What's this stuff?"

I pointed to my plate, where there were three things that looked like purple golf balls.

"Veggie Fabulayerous," he said. "Each one has seven layers. The outside is beets. After that there's broccoli, cauliflower, radishes, brussels sprouts, and peas."

"That sounds disgusting," I said.

"I only counted six layers," Sammy added.

"The Veggie Fabulayerous has a yam filling," my dad said. "That makes seven."

"No offense, Dad, but I don't think kids are going to want to eat these."

Floyd got right up on his plate and sniffed his Veggie Fabulayerous. He rolled one with his paw.

"Ewww," I said.

Floyd started juggling all three Veggie Fabulayerouses, tossed all three into the air, and caught them in his mouth.

"He's like a circus performer," Sammy said. "The kid's got talent."

"Hey, wait," I said. Floyd had a smile on his face and he wasn't spitting them out. "Floyd likes them!"

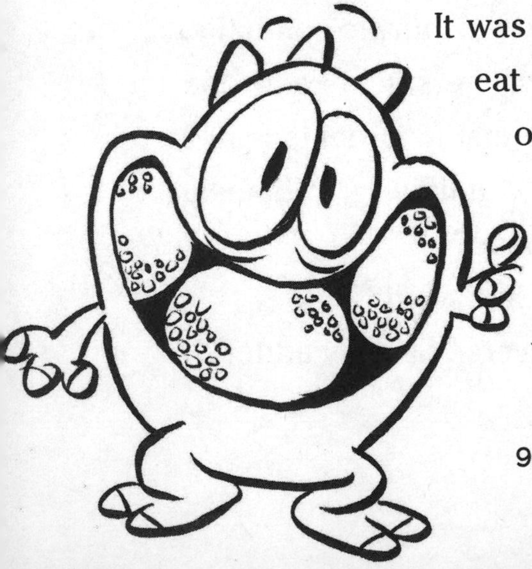

It was true that Floyd would eat anything. He ate one of my shoes once. And a baseball. But still, if Floyd liked this crazy veggie thingamajig, I was willing to try it.

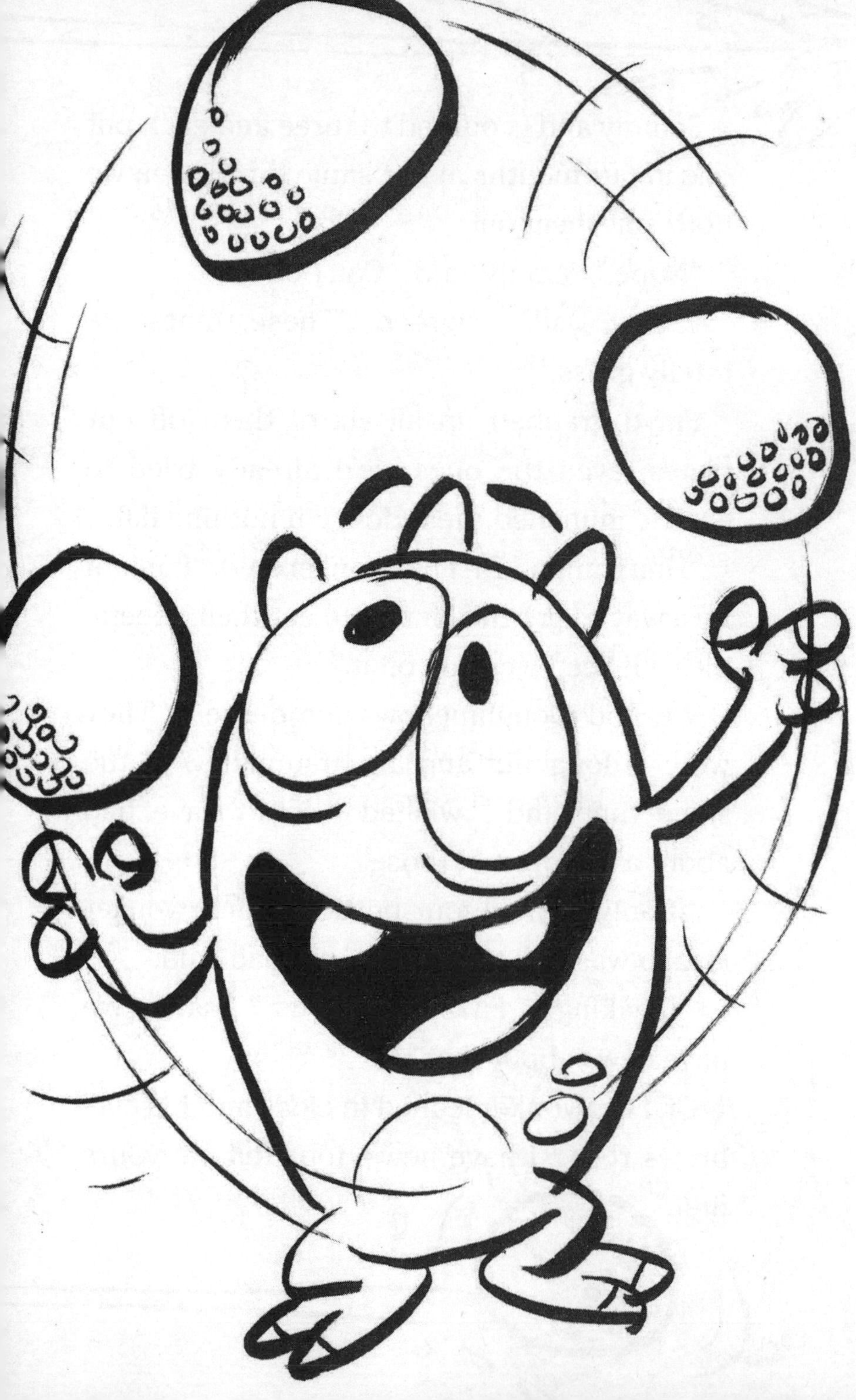

Sammy and I counted to three and each put one in our mouths at the same time. Then we both spit them out.

"Nope," Sammy said. "Can't do it."

"Sorry, Dad," I agreed. "These things are totally gross."

Floyd grabbed up all six of them off our plates, even the ones we'd already tried to eat. He munched them down in nothing flat.

"Hmmmmm," Dr. Fuzzwonker said. "It might be a way to get the Fizzies to eat their vegetables. I'll keep working on it."

We had Doughmellows for dessert. They were a doughnut and a marshmallow at the same time and I wished I could have had about a hundred of those.

"If only we had four bottles of Fuzzwonker Fizz to wash all this down," my dad said.

"Speaking of Fuzzwonker Fizz," I said. "We have news about that."

Dr. Fuzzwonker leaned in close and his eyebrows rose. "I have news, too. Tell me yours first."

I explained everything about the barn full of bottles and the incredible adventure we'd had finding them.

"And Floyd has a plan for how to get the bottles back."

"Do tell," my dad said, then he put a Veggie Fabulayerous in his mouth. About two seconds later he spit it out.

"Okay, here goes," I said. "Floyd thinks he can get all the Fizzies in Fizzopolis together and put them back to work."

"I like the sound of that," Dr. Fuzzwonker said. "They're bored as beans. But what would they do?"

Time to reveal the big plan! "The Fizzies need to dig a tunnel under Pflugerville. It needs to go under all the houses, the Hamburger Shack, the bowling alley, the Pfluger Mart—all of it! And then they need to turn and dig up until they hit the red barn on the Snood property."

Floyd walked on the table until he was standing in front of my dad.

"What's all over your stomach, Floyd?" Dr. Fuzzwonker asked.

"It's a map that shows where the red barn is," Sammy said. "So you can find it."

Dr. Fuzzwonker didn't say anything. I could tell he was doing a million-billion equations in his head, figuring out the math for such a large-scale feat of engineering. It would be a very long tunnel and it would need to be dug fast.

Finally, after a long pause and a bite of his Doughmellow, he gave his answer. "It will be difficult and dangerous. It will take every Fizzy in Fizzopolis. But I do believe this could work."

"Yes!" Sammy yelled.

"We'll begin Operation Fizzy Dig right after we clean up these dishes," Dr. Fuzzwonker said. "But first, I need to explain *this* to you."

Dr. Fuzzwonker carefully pulled a small jar out of his white lab coat pocket. Inside, there was a disk shaped like a tiny Frisbee.

"Is it candy?" I asked.

"Can we eat it?" Sammy asked.

"Absolutely not!" Dr. Fuzzwonker said. "I have broken the Snoodles down to their smallest elements and found that they are sixty-two percent Fuzzwonker Fizz and thirty-one percent Snood's Flooze."

"Dad, that's only ninety-three percent," I reminded him.

"The other seven percent is air."

"What a rip-off!" Sammy said. "There's only ninety-three percent candy in that candy."

"It's diabolical," I agreed.

Dr. Fuzzwonker handed me the jar and explained what was inside. "That, my dear boy, is a Snootralizer. It neutralizes Snoodles."

"It neutra-*whats*?" Sammy said as her nose crinkled up.

"All you need to do is put that Snootralizer into the main vat of material the Snoods are using to make Snoodles. The Snootralizer will render the entire batch burpless, tasteless, and it might have one other side effect."

"What side effect?" I asked.

My dad waved his arm as if it didn't matter. "That's not important now. What is important is that we show those Snoods that they can't use our Fuzzwonker Fizz to make their crummy candy."

"Sounds good to me," Sammy said.

"Me, too," I nodded.

Floyd was sneaking up on my dad's plate,

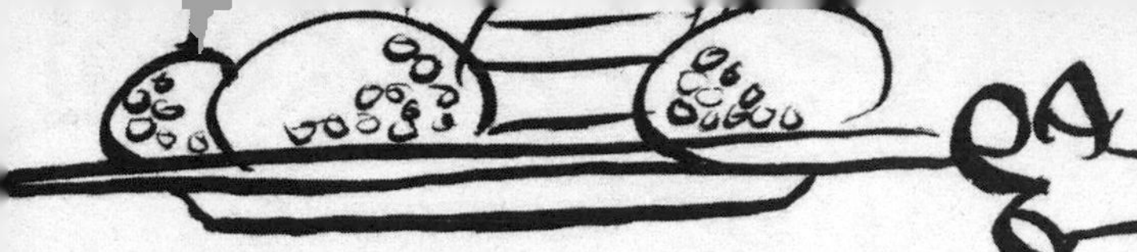

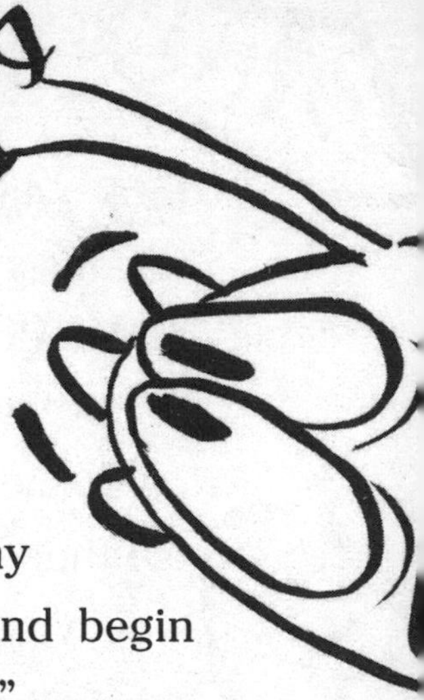

looking to grab the last three Veggie Fabulayerouses.

"We're agreed then," Dr. Fuzzwonker said. "Floyd and I will put Operation Fizzy Dig into action here. Harold, you and Sammy will leave immediately and begin Operation Snootralizer."

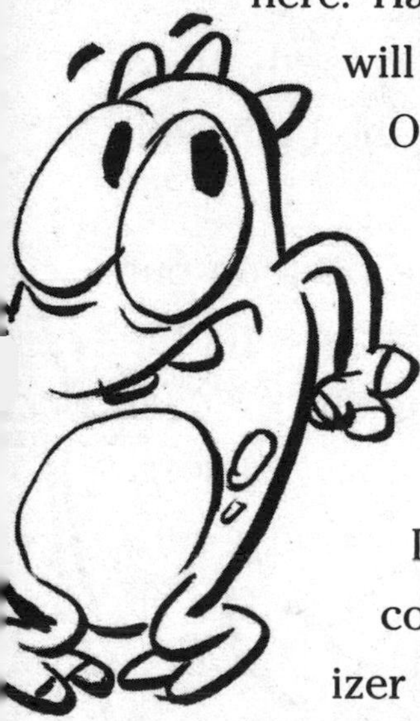

We were about to do something that we'd never tried in the history of Fizzopolis—two operations at one time!

"I only have one request," I said. "I don't think we can complete Operation Snootralizer without taking my best good buddy with me. Now that you've figured out the calculations, could you handle Operation Fizzy Dig without Floyd?"

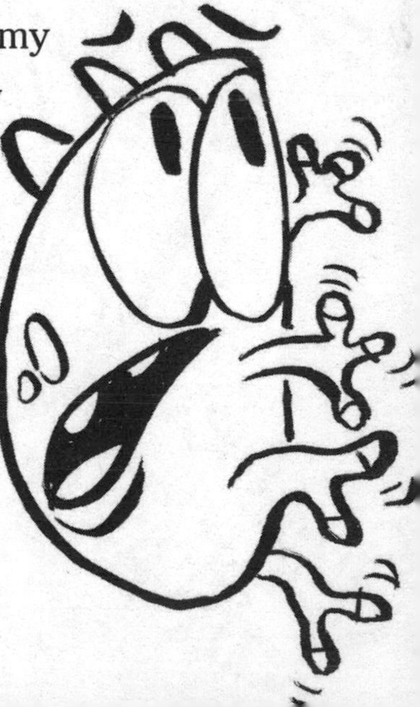

My dad stood up and buttoned his white lab coat. He

took a calculator out of his jacket pocket and furiously tapped keys, then he looked up at us and nodded. "I believe I can."

"Sweet!" Sammy said. "The Fizzy team rides again. Let's blow this weird food joint and finish those Snoodles once and for all."

Floyd landed on my shoulder and talked into my ear. "He needs to use the bathroom first. But then he's good to go."

A few minutes later, we were back on our bikes, racing through Pflugerville with the Snootralizer stored in my backpack.

Summer's GREAT!

HOORAY!! No Homework...

CHAPTER 9

Sammy needed to ride past her house and check in with her parents on the way to the Snoods', so we rode there first.

"Isn't summer great?" she said when she ran back out. "No homework and I can stay out on my bike until late!"

"Summer is definitely the second best invention after Fizzopolis," I said.

"And they're going to call Dr. Fuzzwonker," she said as she got on the Green Pickle and started pedaling. "We're all good for me staying over so we can get the Fizzomatic machine working again."

"What's in the bag?" I asked. Sammy didn't usually ride around Pflugerville with a backpack on.

She smiled mysteriously. "Just stuff we might need. A girl likes to be prepared."

Not only was Sammy my super-duper palomino, she was also super-duper smart. Whatever she had in there was sure to help us out with Operation Snootralizer.

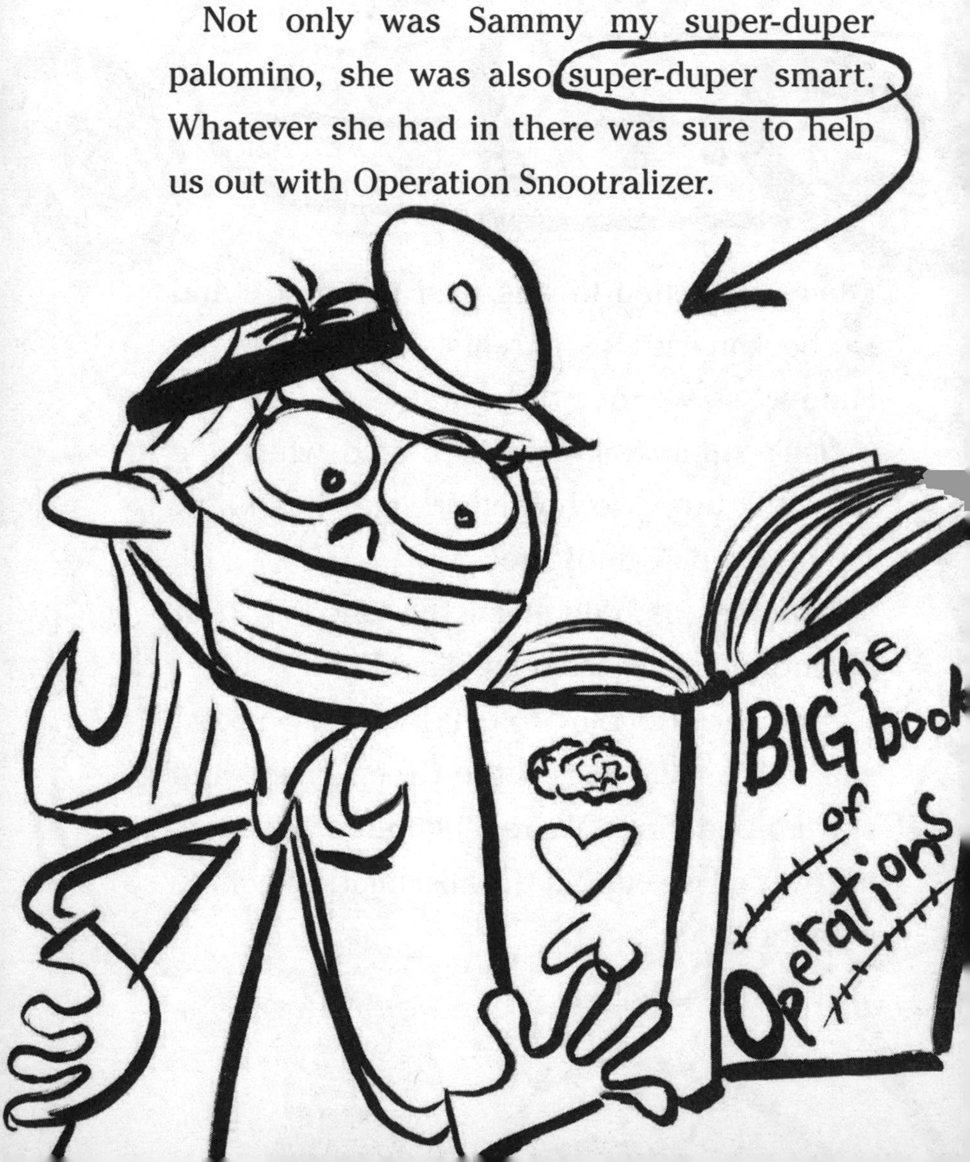
The BIG book of Operations

An hour later the dreamy summer evening showed up and the whole town of Pflugerville was covered in gold light. The sun wasn't going to set for at least a few more hours, so we still had to be on high alert at the Snoods' as we scaled the chicken wire fence for the second time. The blackberry bushes were every bit as sharp as the first time, but it was the only way those dreaded cameras couldn't

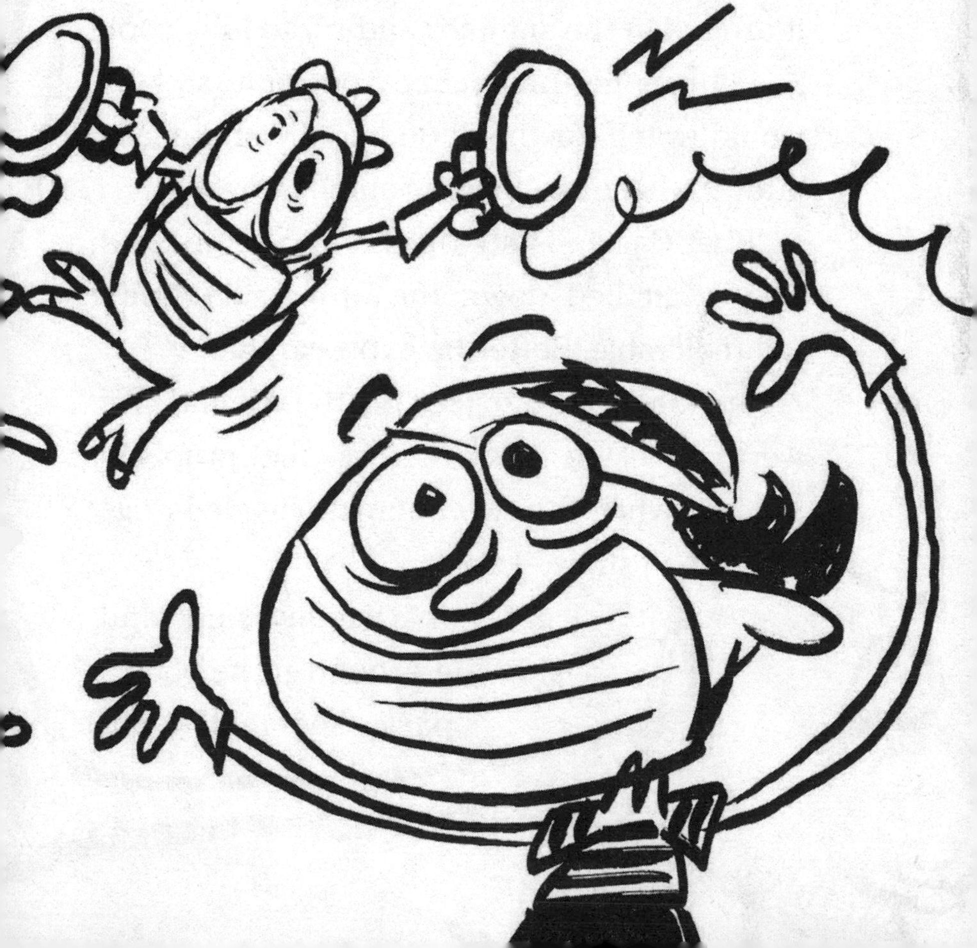

spot us. When we got to the top, it seemed like the Snood Candy Factory was still in high gear making Snoodles.

"The Snoodmobile is gone," I said, pointing to Mr. Snood's vacant parking spot. "This might be easier than we thought."

Mr. Snood's car was the longest one in Pflugerville. It was a pink convertible with whitewall tires, and Mr. Snood liked to drive it around in the summer and try to look cool. Sometimes he threw candy out of it, so kids would watch for the Snoodmobile and chase after it whenever he was running errands.

"I bet Garvin is still in there," Sammy said as we climbed down the other side. "He's unpredictable. Better be extra careful."

I nodded and our feet hit the ground. We were about to start across the property when the two pumpkin-headed dogs showed up.

"I got this," Sammy said, and she dug around in her backpack. She pulled out

two of the biggest
dog treats I'd ever seen.
They were like dinosaur bones.
"These should keep them busy for
a while."

"Sammy, you're brilliant!" I said as Floyd
hopped onto my shoulder. "Also Floyd would
like one of those bones."

Sammy shook her head and threw her
backpack on again. "Sorry, Floyd. Right now
we're on a secret mission. Snacks will have
to wait."

Floyd grumbled and stuck his finger in my
ear just to be ornery.

The dogs struggled to drag their treats
away and we were on the move again. But I
didn't know where we were going next. I didn't
really have a plan for getting inside the Snood
Candy Factory.

"Follow me, guys," Sammy said. She headed
for the back side of the candy factory, and I
followed her. Floyd asked me where she was
going.

"I have no idea."

Floyd said we should follow her so he could put Operation Get-Floyd-a-Treat into action.

"We can't handle three operations at once!" I said. "Two is our limit, little buddy."

Floyd grumbled some more and then we arrived at the ladder leading up to the roof for the second time that day.

"What are we going to do up there?" I asked Sammy. She went first this time and I climbed up behind her. "Shouldn't we try that crazy doggy door? That worked once before."

"With all this added security, there's no way that darn doggy door is going to work

this time. We need a new way in." (If you don't know about the doggy door, it's in my first journal, *The Trouble with Fuzzwonker Fizz.* Look it up, newbie.)

Once we got on the roof, I could see all of Pflugerville. I pulled out my binoculars and scanned the town. Miss Yoobler was sitting in a lawn chair sipping a drink with an umbrella in it. Cars pulled in and out of Mo's bowling alley. The Hamburger Shack was hopping.

"Uh-oh," I said.

"What do you see?" Sammy asked nervously.

"The Snoodmobile is leaving the Hamburger Shack. It's heading this way!"

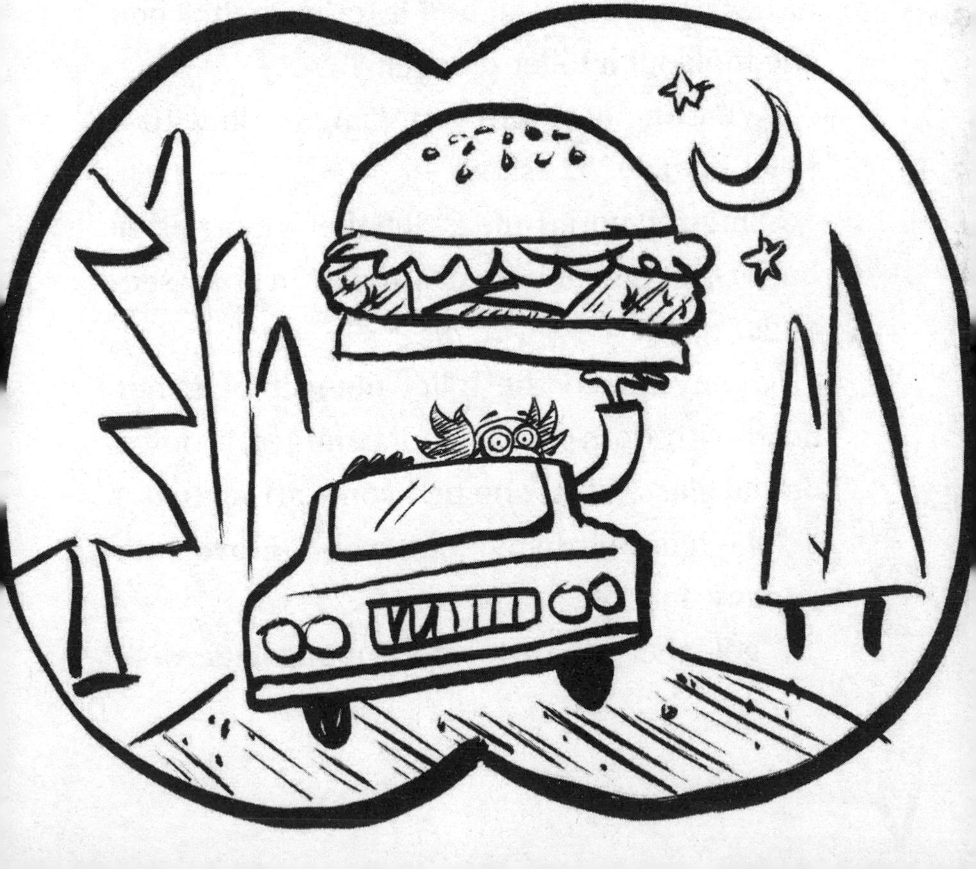

Sammy took her backpack off and dug her hand inside. Out came a spy watch. She played around with the settings. "Looks like we've got about six minutes before Mr. Snood shows up here with Pfluger burgers. We need to hurry."

I put the binoculars in my backpack and Sammy went to the skylight. It was incredibly thick glass, so I figured there was no way to break through it. Sammy took something out of her pack and attached it to her belt. Then she took out a toilet plunger.

"What the heck are you going to do with a toilet plunger?" I asked.

Sammy ignored me. "Get the Snootralizer out of that jar. I'll be ready to roll in sixty seconds."

Sammy raised the toilet plunger over her head with both hands and slammed it down on the glass. Then she tied some string to it.

"She has weird spy equipment," Floyd said into my ear.

I got the jar with the Snootralizer disk

and tried to get the top off. It was really on there. My face turned red and I rolled around on the roof trying to get that darn thing off. Floyd took it from me and jumped about ten feet into the air. He held the jar with his little paws and bashed it into the roof, but the glass didn't break. Floyd hit that jar against the roof about a hundred times and then he gave up.

"Sammy, I think we have a problem," I said as I turned and looked at her. "Hey! Wow, how'd you do that?"

Sammy had cut a perfectly round hole in the glass, which was big enough to fit through. She stood over the opening holding the toilet plunger with a round piece of glass stuck to it. "It's amazing what you can do with a plunger, a piece of string, and a glass-cutting stone."

"That's awesome sauce!" I said. I looked at the jar in my hand. "Now back to my problem. I can't get this jar open. It's impossible."

Sammy set the toilet plunger down and held out her hand, so I gave her the jar. She spun the lid right off.

"What the?" I yelled. "That's also impossible!"

Sammy shrugged like it was no big deal. "You must have loosened it. Either that or I'm a lot stronger than you are."

She giggled.

"No doubt about it," I agreed as I looked at my noodle arm. "I definitely loosened it."

Sammy took the Snootralizer disk out of the jar and tucked it into her belt while Floyd and I went to the skylight and looked down into the hole she'd cut out.

The top of the Snood Candy Factory was one of the tallest places in Pflugerville.

Garvin was below, driving around on the forklift. He looked like an ant. "It's a long way down there."

Sammy pulled a line of cable from her belt and attached it to the smokestack, which was about ten feet away from the skylight. She came over and stood next to me. "No problemo."

"You have way better spy gear than I do," I said.

She looked at her spy watch. "T-minus sixty seconds before Mr. Snood arrives with the Pfluger burgers. It's go time."

I took another look down at the factory floor. The giant tub full of Snoodles was bubbling like a boiling vat of oil. It was way over to the left of where we were standing. "You'll need to sidearm that Snootralizer disk and aim it like a pro. You can do it, Sammy."

Floyd jumped on her shoulder and folded his arms like he wasn't taking no for an answer. "He's not letting you go alone," I said. "You need a travel buddy."

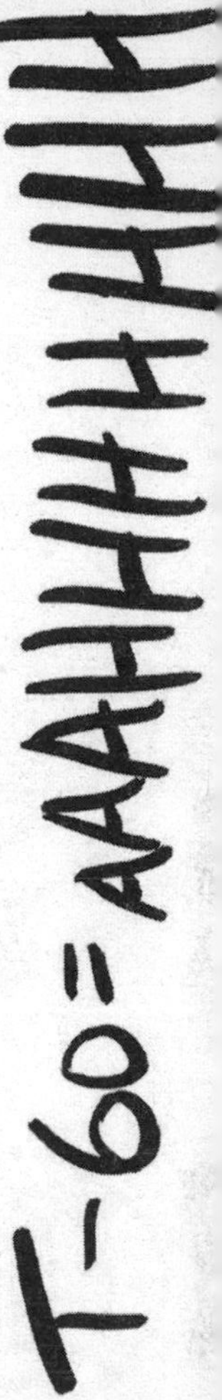
T-60 = AAHHHHHH

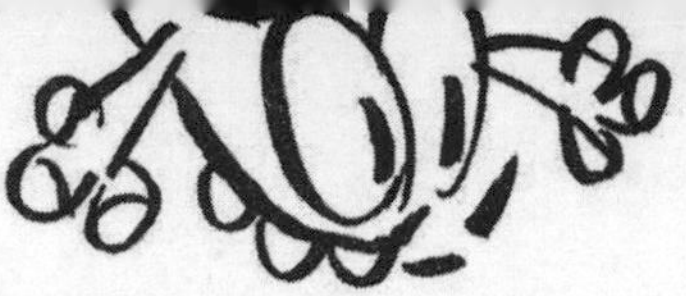

Floyd nodded bravely and then Sammy lowered herself into the hole. Down she went with a zipping sound that got softer and softer. She ran out of cable about halfway down and jerked to a stop.

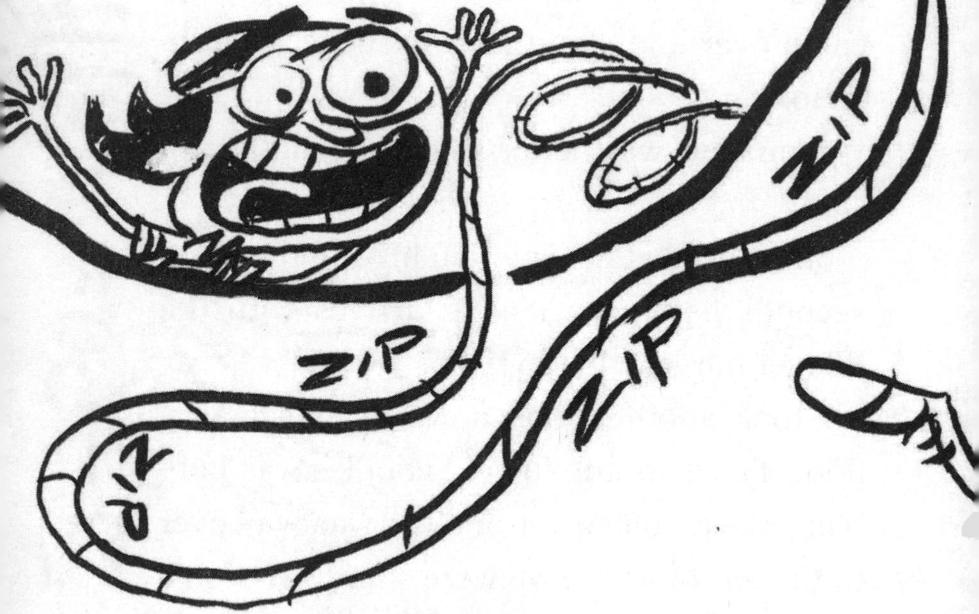
ZIP
ZIP
ZIP
ZIP

She'd stopped short of where she'd hoped and the vat of Snoodles stuff was blocked by a conveyor belt.

"Swing me!" Sammy shouted up in my direction, so I reached my arm down

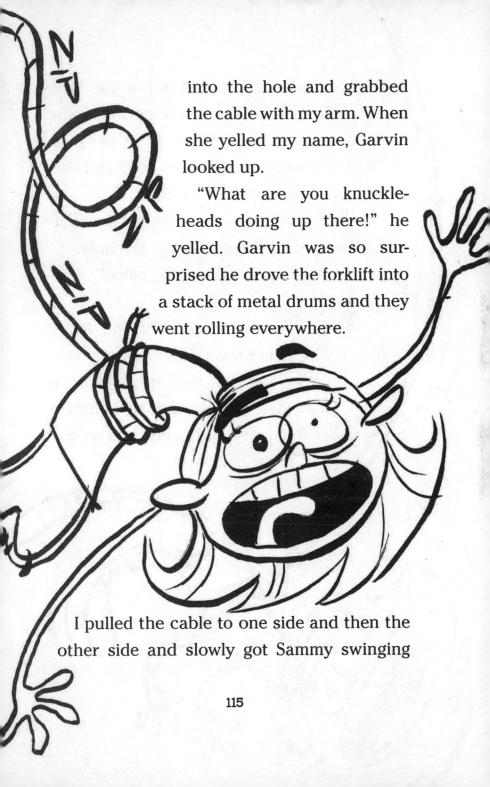

into the hole and grabbed the cable with my arm. When she yelled my name, Garvin looked up.

"What are you knuckle-heads doing up there!" he yelled. Garvin was so surprised he drove the forklift into a stack of metal drums and they went rolling everywhere.

I pulled the cable to one side and then the other side and slowly got Sammy swinging

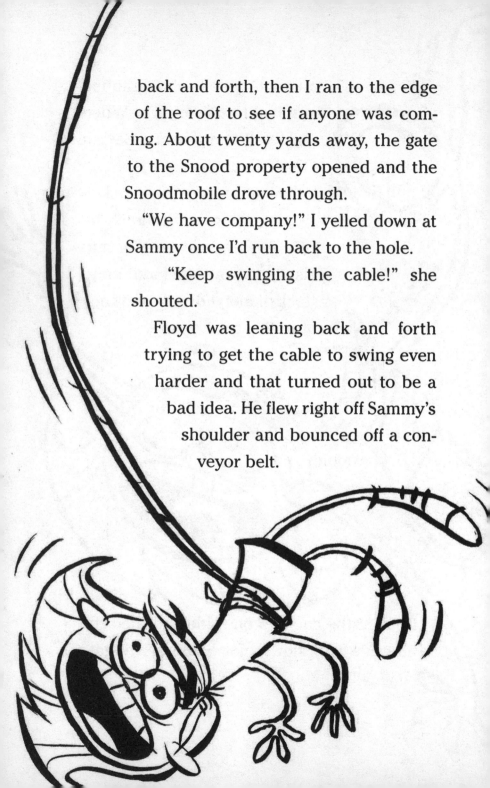

back and forth, then I ran to the edge of the roof to see if anyone was coming. About twenty yards away, the gate to the Snood property opened and the Snoodmobile drove through.

"We have company!" I yelled down at Sammy once I'd run back to the hole.

"Keep swinging the cable!" she shouted.

Floyd was leaning back and forth trying to get the cable to swing even harder and that turned out to be a bad idea. He flew right off Sammy's shoulder and bounced off a conveyor belt.

"Floyd!" I yelled.

"You losers are in big trouble!" Garvin said. He kept driving the forklift until he arrived at the front door of the factory. Then he jumped off and fled the building.

"Operation Snootralizer is in double trouble!" I shouted, but I kept swinging the cable anyway. Floyd bounced off two more conveyor belts and landed on top of the forklift.

"Don't do it, Floyd!" I said, because I knew Floyd would want to drive that crazy thing. Sure enough, he dropped down onto the driver's seat and started looking for the on switch.

"That's enough swing!" Sammy yelled up at me. She was flying back and forth like a pendulum, holding the Snootralizer in one hand. I ran to the edge of the roof and looked down.

The Snoods were coming up the ladder!

I ran back toward the skylight and tripped on my shoelace. Talk about a face-plant. But I got back to the hole in time to see Sammy sidearm the Snootralizer and watch it land in the vat of Snoodles goop. It bubbled more than it was bubbling before. It turned orange, then purple, then back to yellow.

"Nice shot, Sammy!" I yelled. "Not to bum you out, but the Snoods are almost to the roof!"

"That's perfect," she said.

"It is?"

"Come on down. We'll take the fork-lift. Floyd's already got it started."

"Sweet!"

I slid down the cable, and my hands got so hot they practically started smoking. I was moving way too fast when I arrived at Sammy's head, and when we connected, the cable snapped.

"AAAAaaYYyaaaaYyaaaayayay-aaaAAaaaaAAAAAAAaaaaaa!" We both screamed as we tumbled and bounced off all sorts of stuff on the way down. We hit conveyer belts. We hit cables. We hit nets and boxes and robot arms. And then we hit the floor of the factory.

"That didn't feel great," Sammy said. "Are you okay?"

I had some bumps and bruises, but I was fine. "I'm good. You?"

She looked up, so I did, too. Garvin and his dad were staring down at us from the hole in the skylight. They were both eating Pfluger burgers.

"Don't move!" Mr. Snood said. "We're coming down there this instant!"

I looked at Sammy. "Should we listen to him?"

Floyd was driving the forklift around, bumping into things like a maniac.

"We better help Floyd instead," Sammy said. "How are we going to get out of here?"

I had a brilliant idea about how to finish off Operation Snootralizer.

"Come on," I said. "Let's climb aboard that forklift!"

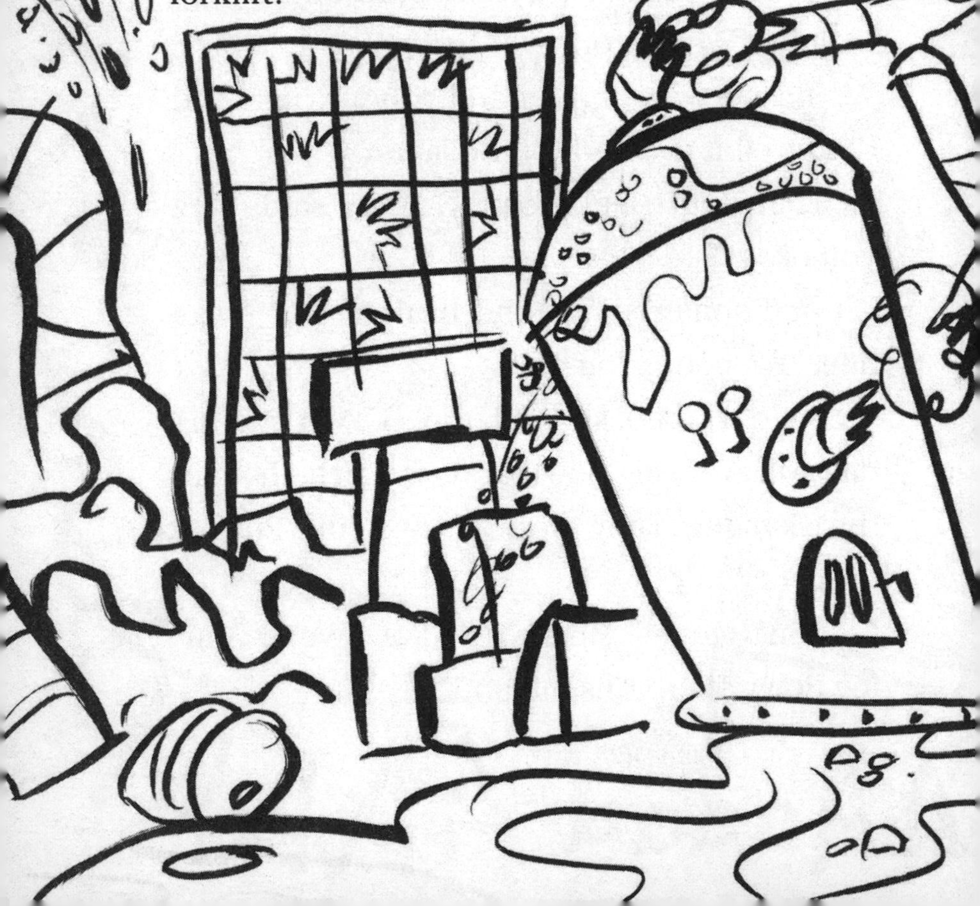

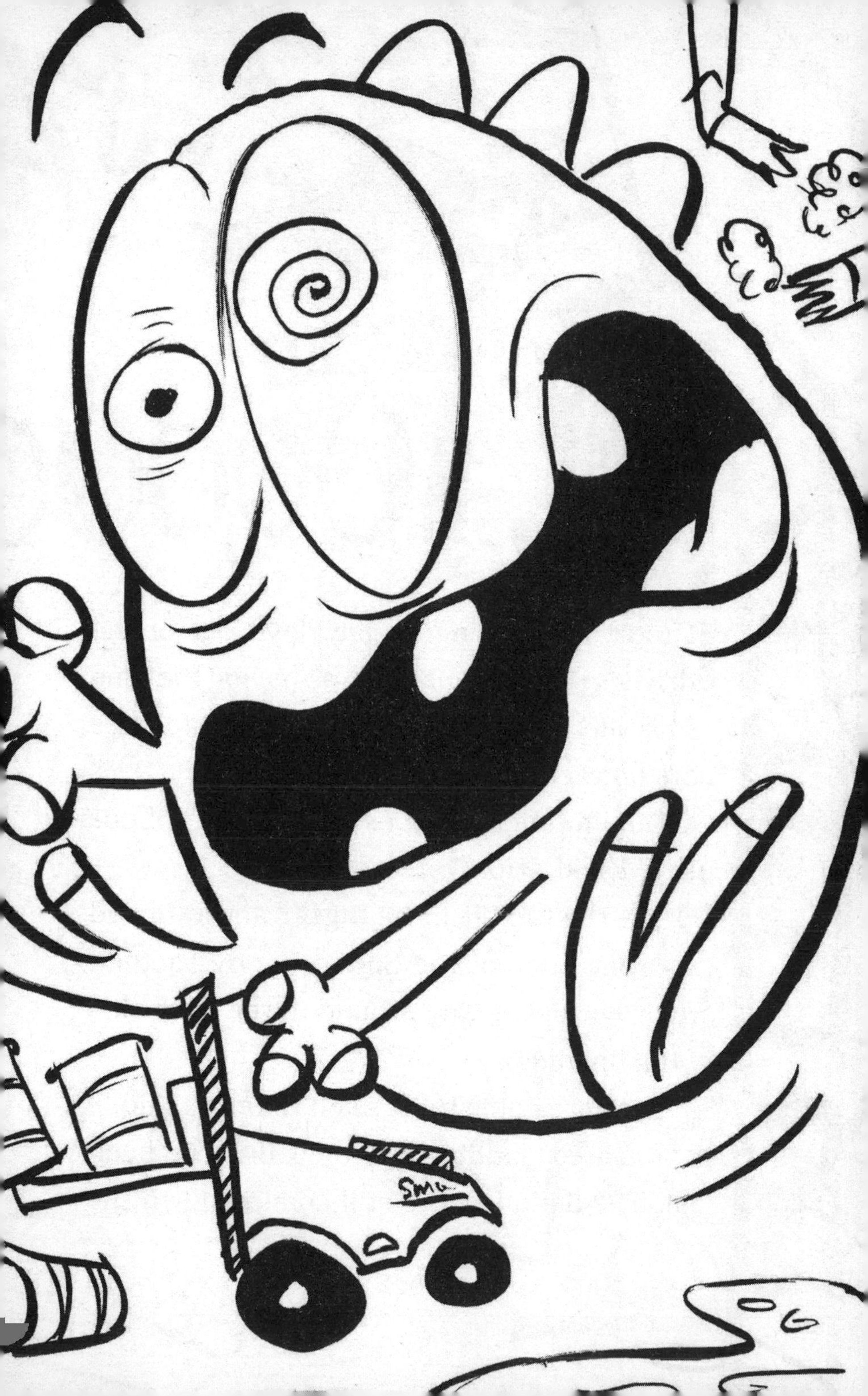
SMG

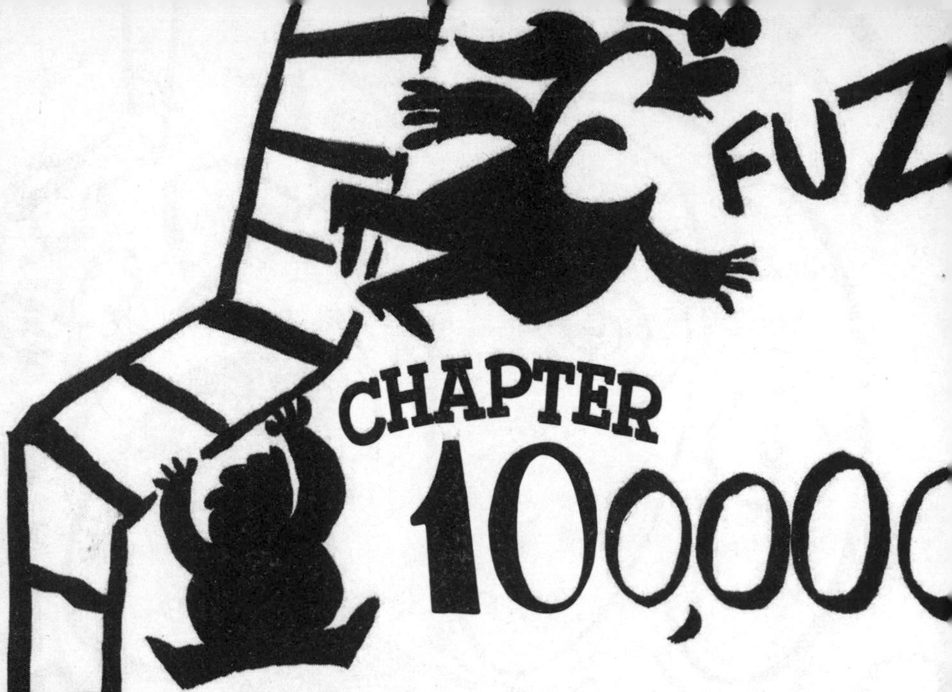
FUZ

CHAPTER 10,000

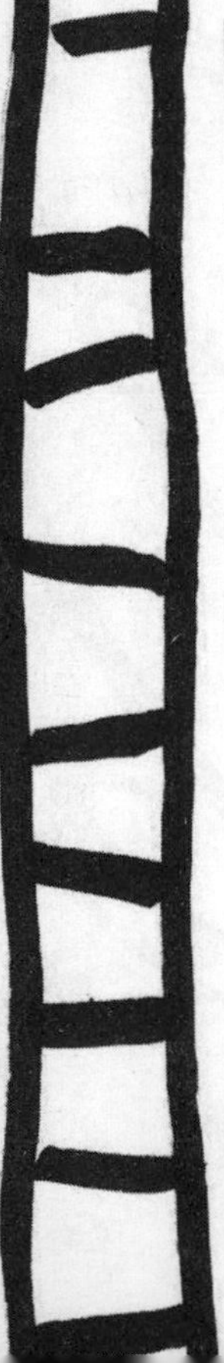

It took some doing to get Floyd out of the driver's seat, because he was having the time of his life. I had to bribe him with Snoodles bars I picked up from the factory floor.

"Time to initiate the escape portion of our plan," I said. "Hold on, everyone!"

I put the forklift in high gear and rammed the front door of the Snood Candy Factory. We drove all the way around to the back side of the building.

"They are going to be mad!" Sammy said.

"You aren't kidding," I agreed. But we'd been fast. The Snoods were still coming down the

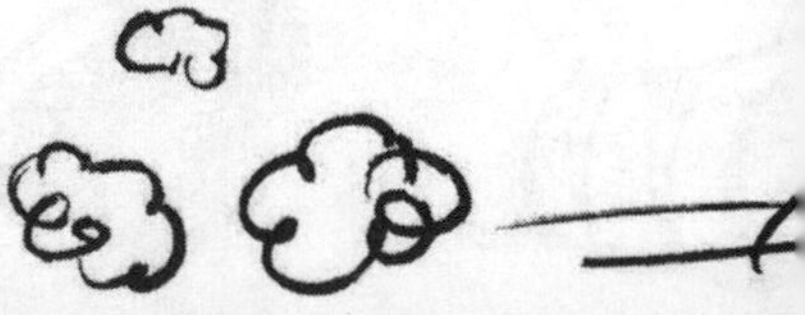

ladder as we drove right past them.

"Harold Fuzzwonkeeeeeeeeeer!" Mr. Snood yelled.

"You're going the wrong way," Sammy said, pointing to the chicken wire fence. "Our bikes are over there."

"We're not going that way," I said with a sly grin, and I gunned the forklift into the woods.

Even at top speed, the forklift was nowhere near as fast as the Snoodmobile. They'd catch us for sure.

"Floyd, I need you to change up these signs. Are you with me?" I asked.

Floyd gave me a salute. He was ready for duty. At each sign we passed in the woods, he jumped up and spun them in different directions. It was confusing out there, with so many paths to take. It was sure to slow the Snoodmobile down as they came searching for us.

We followed the signs for the red barn, turning them in the wrong direction whenever we passed them, and arrived in the clearing with the sun just starting to set.

"What a sunset," Sammy said. "Boy, do I love summer."

"Come on! Let's hope Operation Fizzy Dig is going as well as Operation Snootralizer."

We jumped off the forklift and ran to the red barn. There was a padlock on the door, but Sammy came to the rescue again. She had a lock-picking tool out in a flash.

"You're the best spy I've ever seen in my life!" I said. "Your new nickname is 007."

"Thanks, Harold. You're pretty great, too."

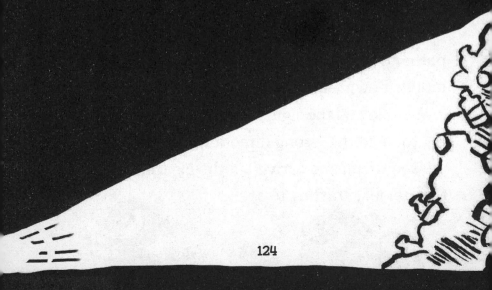

The lock popped open and we slowly creaked the door inward. It was dark in there, so I took the flashlight out of my backpack and turned it on. A beam of white light shot through the darkness.

"Bummer," I said.

The incredibly gigantic pile of Fuzzwonker Fizz bottles was still sitting there. "The Snoods are going to be here any minute," Sammy said. "We'll be trapped in here."

I was fresh out of ideas. Somehow I'd

thought that the bottles would be gone and we could climb down the big tunnel and find our way back to Fizzopolis. I was bummed out, so Floyd gave me a head hug. He wrapped his arms and legs around the side of my noggin. I felt a little better.

"Someone is coming!" Sammy said. She bolted for the door and peeked out. "The Snoodmobile is almost here!"

Sammy sprang into action while Floyd kept hugging my head. She grabbed two

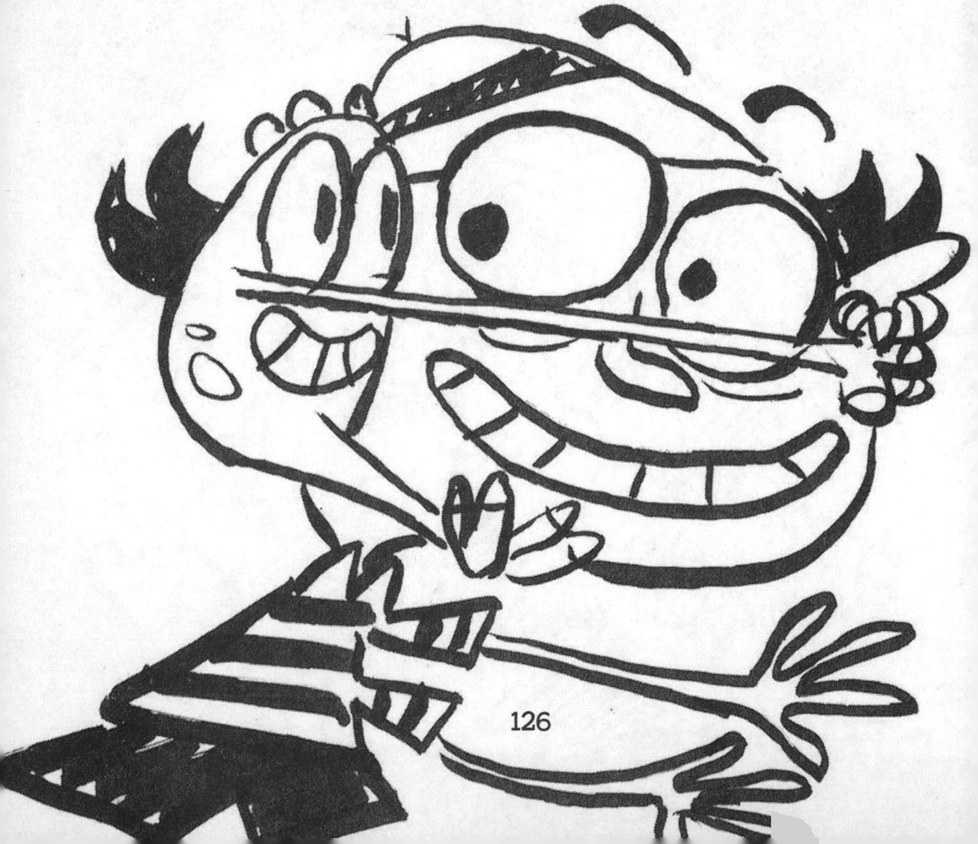

Fuzzwonker Fizz bottles and jammed them under the door so it couldn't swing open.

"That should keep them out, but not for long," Sammy said. "What are we going to do?"

And then something miraculous happened.

"Do you guys feel that?" Sammy asked.

All I could feel were Floyd's legs jammed into my neck and his paw stuck in my eye.

"Floyd, I'm feeling better. You can let go now."

Once Floyd let go, I felt it, too.

The ground was shaking.

"Boy, that Snoodmobile really packs a wallop," I said.

"Has Pflugerville ever had an earthquake?" Sammy asked as the bottles rattled together. Some of them tumbled off the top and landed by our feet.

I heard the car doors shut outside the barn, and then the Snoods were at the door, trying to push it open. Boy, were they mad.

The ground was still shaking, and that's when I figured out it wasn't the crazy rumbling of the Snoodmobile or an earthquake.

"It's Operation Fizzy Dig!" I yelled.

The whole barn shook and the ground near our feet gave way.

"Back up!" I shouted. "These bottles are about to fall into a giant hole!"

The whole pile of one hundred thousand bottles started to disappear. It began in the very middle and moved out to the edges until the sound was so loud we had to cover our ears.

"It's working!" Sammy yelled.

The barn kept shaking and the bottles kept clanging and pretty soon there was nothing left but a giant hole in the ground. We could

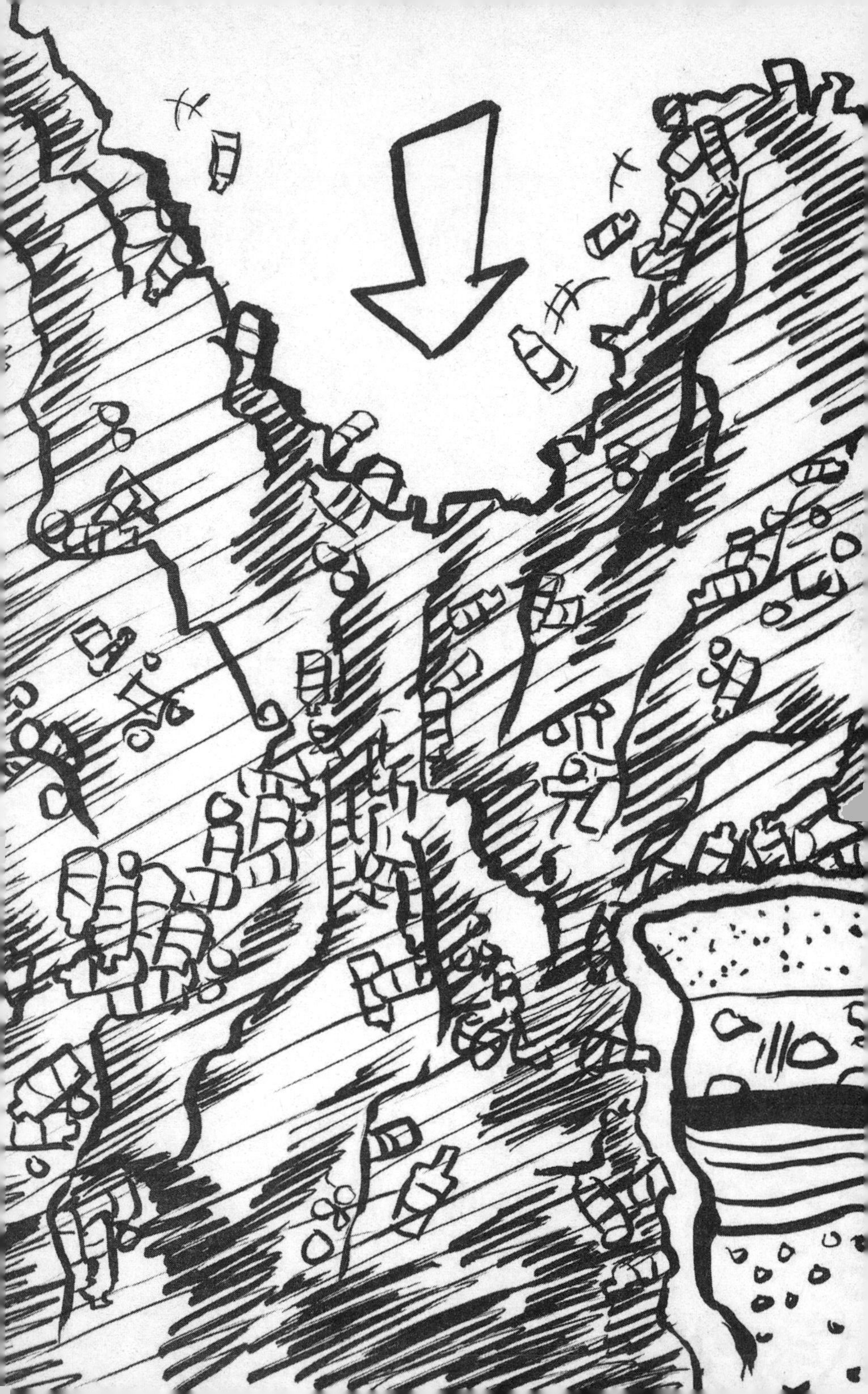

hear the bottles rolling down toward Fizzopolis, echoing quieter and quieter.

"I can't believe that actually worked," I said. "Floyd, you're a genius!"

Floyd beamed.

"LET US IN THERE!" Mr. Snood screamed. The only two Fuzzwonker Fizz bottles left in the whole place were holding the door firmly shut.

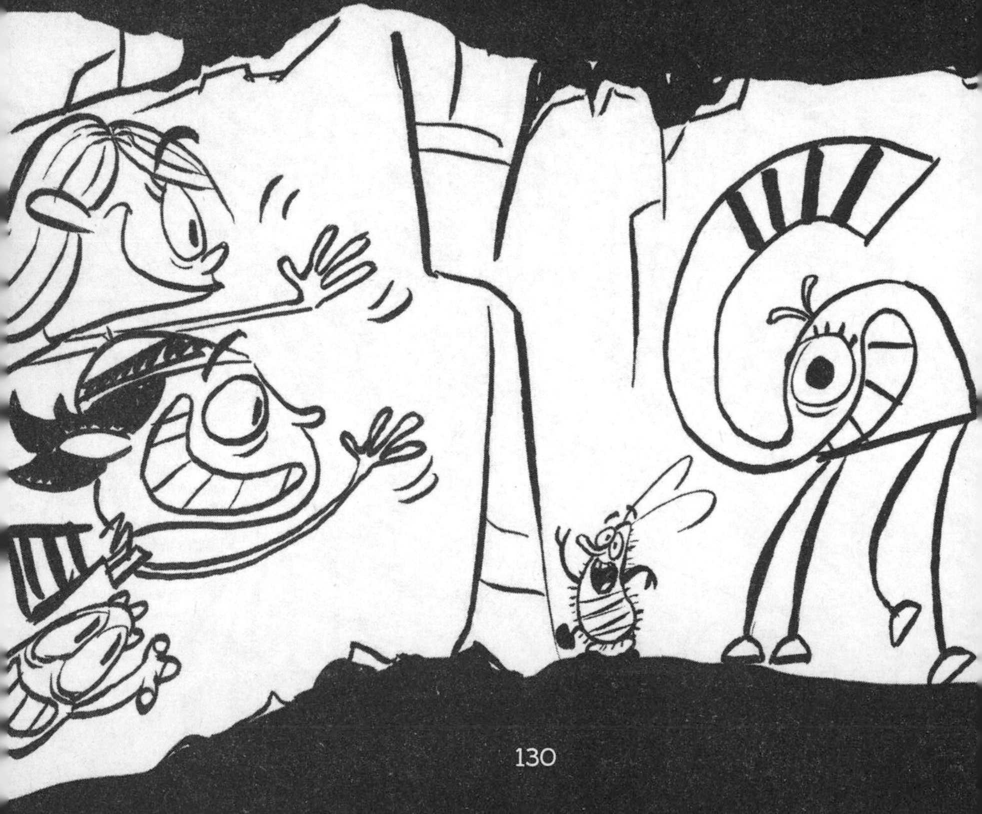

A commotion followed from down in the hole and when we peeked over the edge we saw lights dancing toward us. A few seconds later, Dr. Fuzzwonker appeared among a pack of Fizzies. Grabstack led the way, followed by Franny and George and a bunch of other Fizzies.

"Hey, Dad!" I said, waving into the hole. "Great job with Operation Fizzy Dig."

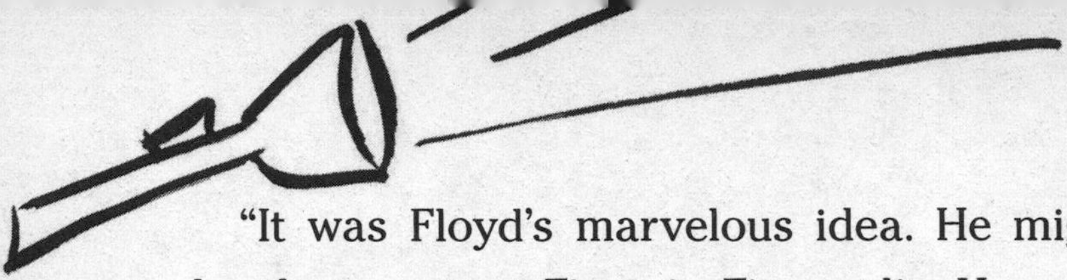

"It was Floyd's marvelous idea. He might be the smartest Fizzy in Fizzopolis. How did Operation Snootralizer go?"

"We had a few bumps along the way, but Sammy saved the day. She's a super spy."

"I'm not surprised," Dr. Fuzzwonker said. "Jump down here with us and we'll take the tunnel back to Fizzopolis."

Sammy and I slid down the side of the hole and landed in a pile of Fizzies. Good thing they're super soft and furry.

"The Snoods will be here any second," Sammy said. "If they find this hole, they'll follow it right to Fizzopolis."

I hadn't thought of that. Oops.

"Fizzy team two, you're up!" Dr. Fuzzwonker said.

All the Fizzies standing around us flew into action. There were about fifty of them, and half started digging a second tunnel off the first one.

"It's a two-tunnel job," my dad said. "Gotta have backfill."

We moved down the tunnel about fifty feet and watched as the Fizzies went to work.

"Commence backfill!" Dr. Fuzzwonker's voice boomed.

"Wow," Sammy said. "They're fast."

"When Fizzies want to dig, they can really dig," my dad said. "How else do you think Fizzopolis got so big?"

Before I could say *that's great, Dad!* the hole was completely covered and we were moving down the tunnel with our flashlight. If you've never followed an underground tunnel for a mile and a half with a flashlight, you have to try it. The whole way back we all kept wondering what it must have been like for the Snoods to open that barn door.

"All those Fuzzwonker Fizz bottles vanished," Sammy said. "Poof. Like magic."

"How cool is that?" I asked. "And now we can make more Fuzzwonker Fizz!"

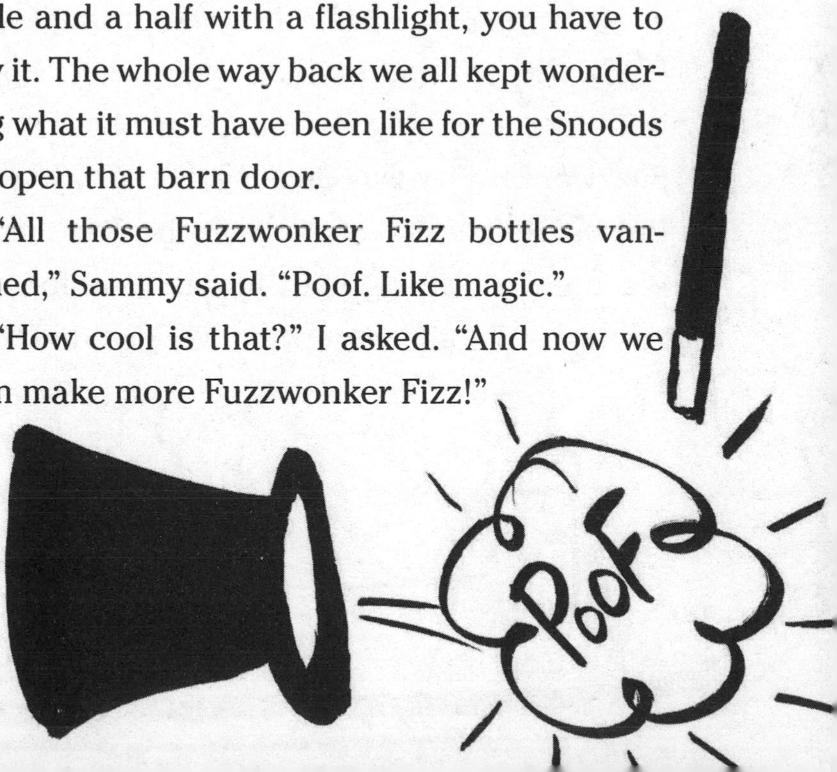
Poof

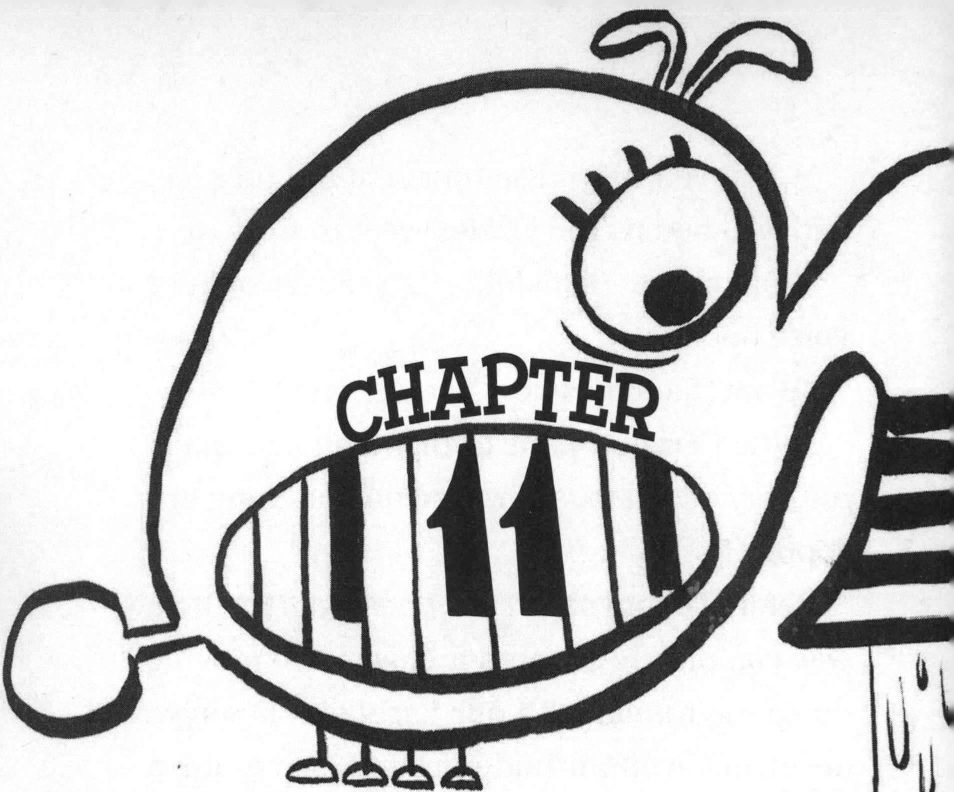

CHAPTER 11

After we put all the bottles through the bottle-washing system, they were loaded into the assembly line and production of Fuzzwonker Fizz was once again ready to roll. But before my dad started up the Fizzomatic machine, we all decided it was time for the Fizzies vs. Food competition. We decided that

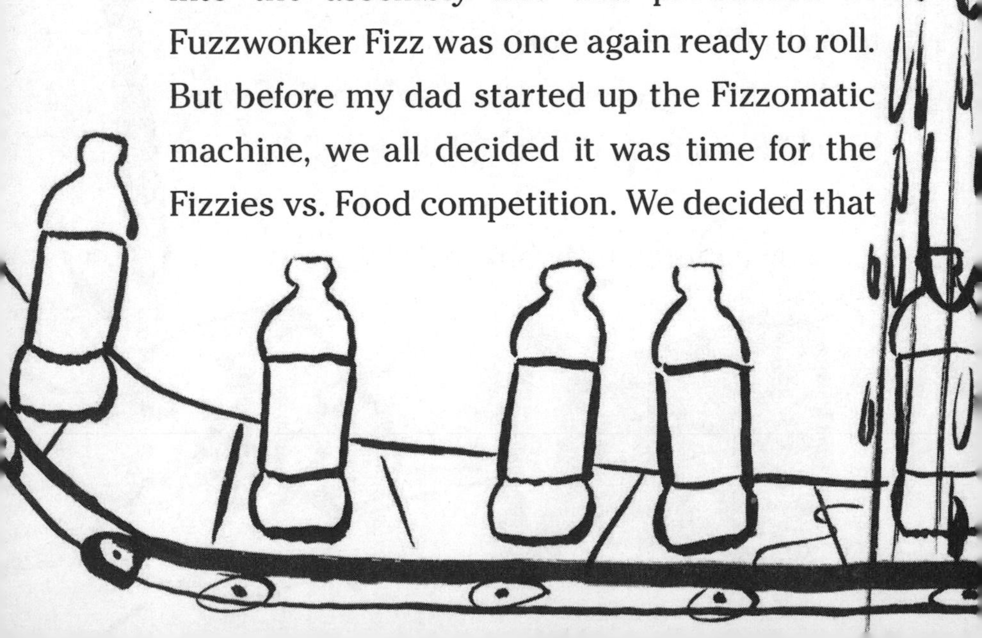

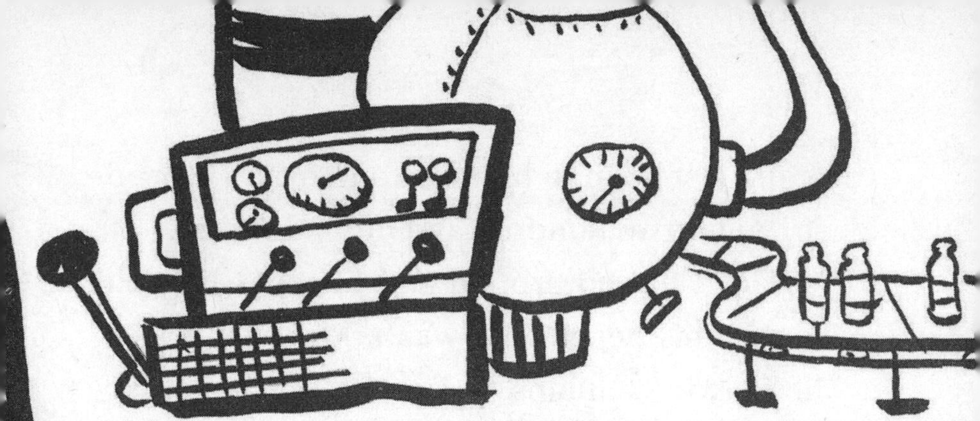

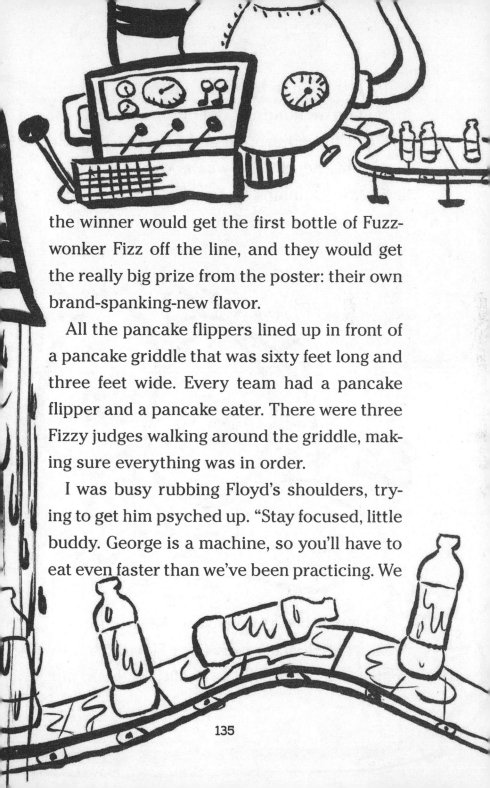

the winner would get the first bottle of Fuzzwonker Fizz off the line, and they would get the really big prize from the poster: their own brand-spanking-new flavor.

All the pancake flippers lined up in front of a pancake griddle that was sixty feet long and three feet wide. Every team had a pancake flipper and a pancake eater. There were three Fizzy judges walking around the griddle, making sure everything was in order.

I was busy rubbing Floyd's shoulders, trying to get him psyched up. "Stay focused, little buddy. George is a machine, so you'll have to eat even faster than we've been practicing. We

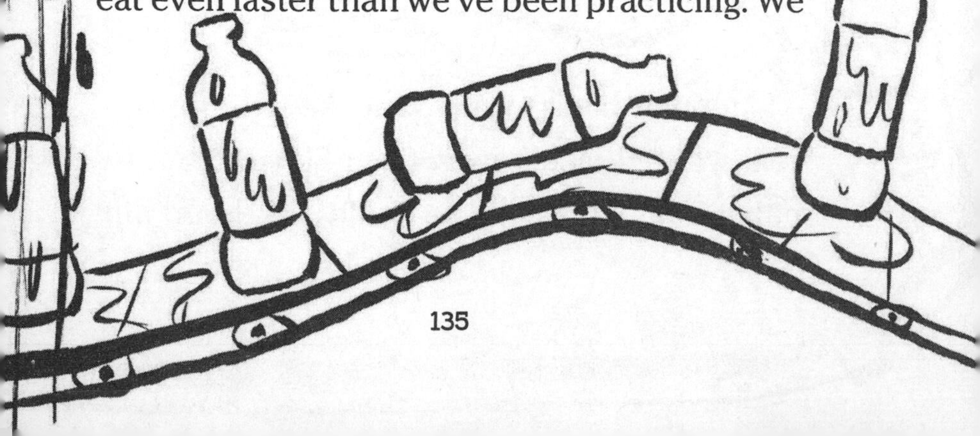

can't just go for a hundred and fifty. We need to go for two hundred and fifty pancakes."

Floyd turned around and his eyes bugged out of his head. That was a lot of pancakes in only ten minutes. Sammy stepped over for moral support. "You can do it, Floyd. Imagine getting to have your own name on a Fuzz-wonker Fizz bottle. I believe in you!"

I stepped back to my pancake flipping station, where I faced away from Floyd. I had to make them as fast as he could eat them, flip them over my head, and aim them into his mouth. We'd practiced this a million times, but I was still nervous. There was no room for errors. I couldn't spill any pancake batter or flip one over his head, which would be easy to do because he was by far the smallest Fizzy in the competition.

To my left, there were a whole line of Fizzies getting ready to pour and flip. Some of them had way more than two arms, so that was going to make it even tougher. To my right, the same thing, including my dad. His partner was Franny, who had once been filled with thousands of gallons of Fuzzwonker Fizz. She was big competition. Franny could probably hold ten thousand pancakes, but I didn't think my dad could flip them faster than I could. Besides, what kind of Fuzzwonker Fizz would Franny even have? She was the swamp cleaner. Franny's Disgusting Sludge flavor? No way! We had to win this thing.

"On your marks," Sammy said. She was smiling from ear to ear. "Get set."

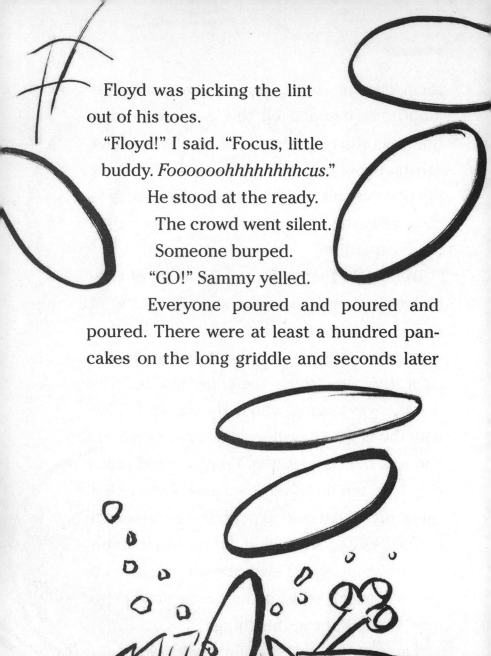

Floyd was picking the lint out of his toes.

"Floyd!" I said. "Focus, little buddy. *Foooooohhhhhhhhcus.*"

He stood at the ready.

The crowd went silent.

Someone burped.

"GO!" Sammy yelled.

Everyone poured and poured and poured. There were at least a hundred pancakes on the long griddle and seconds later they were flipping in the air to cook the other side. There was a lot of sizzling sounds and all of Fizzopolis smelled like breakfast.

"Incoming!" I yelled, and the first three pancakes went airborne over my head. I heard Floyd munching as pancakes fell like rain all across the competition. Then I was pouring again. The race was on!

What transpired in Fizzopolis

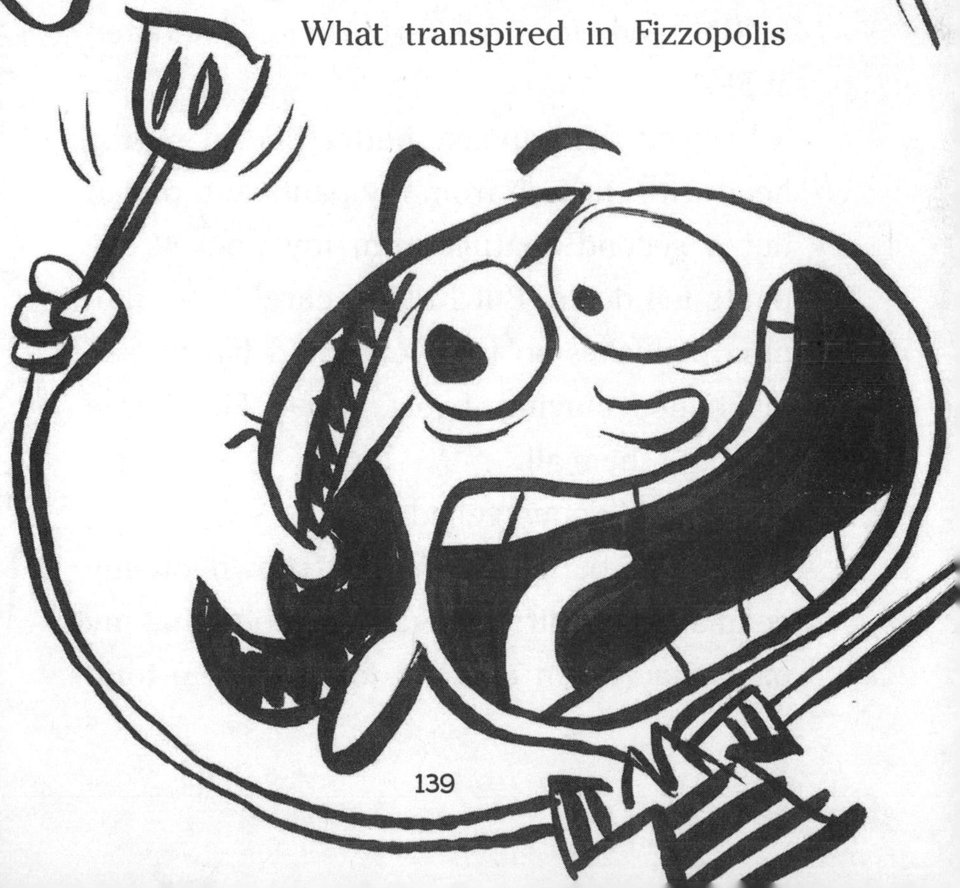

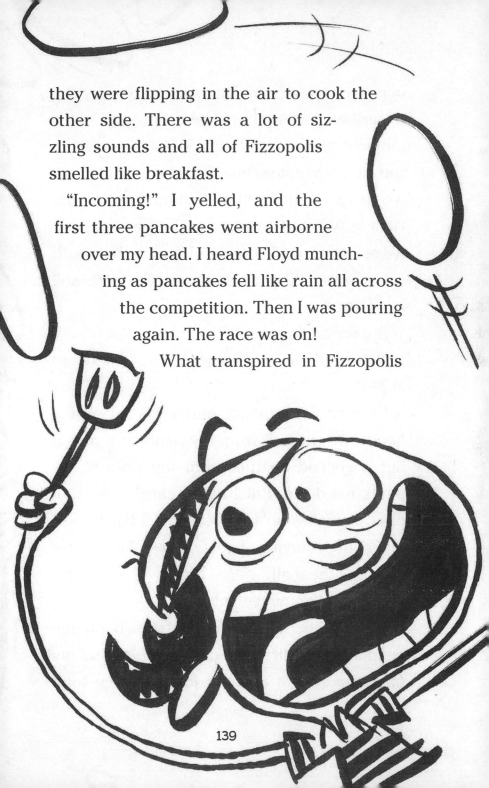

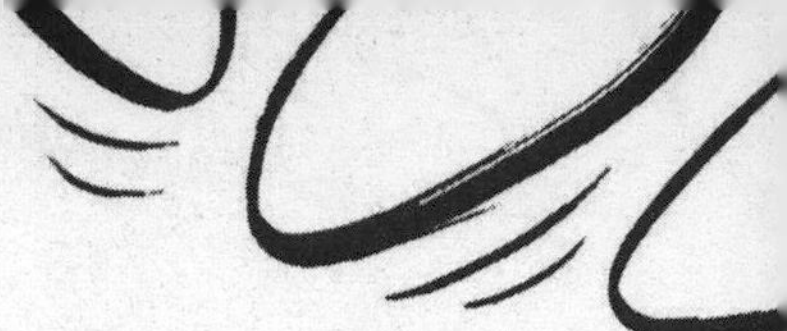

over the next ten minutes can only be described as total mayhem. At any given moment, there were hundreds of pancakes in the air at the same time. By the halfway point, we were in third place behind Franny and George. We had to pick up the pace or we'd never catch up. George and Franny had both eaten over 120 pancakes and we were still stuck at 96.

But we had a plan.

"Get ready for the afterburners!" I shouted at Floyd.

I rigged the pancake batter bucket on my head with the belt from my pants and pulled out a second spatula from my pocket. My pants fell down. But I didn't care! I was flipping pancakes so fast you could hardly see my hands moving. I just hoped Floyd was catching them all.

"TIME!" Sammy yelled.

A lot of batter had spilled down on my head and my shirt. And did I mention that my pants had fallen down? I looked like a total

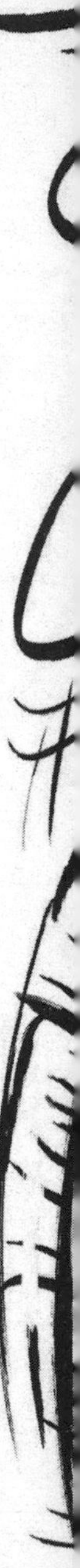

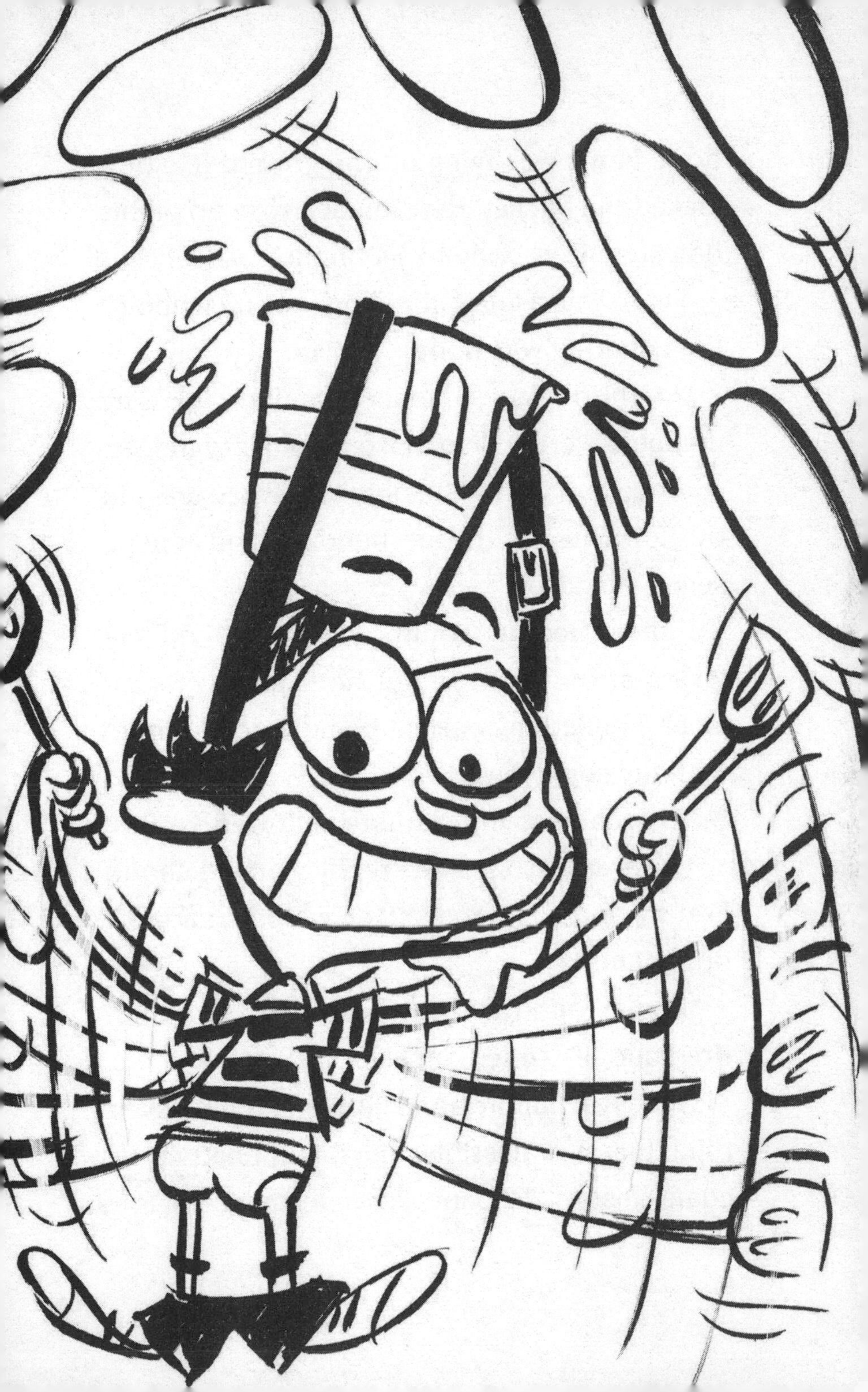

dork. Floyd was lying on the ground like he'd kicked the bucket. His stomach rose up off his hamster-sized body like a blimp.

There was a lot of standing around while all the counting was done.

"In third place," Sammy finally said. The numbers were rolling in from the Fizzy judges. "George and Bob—the only two-Fizzy team in the top three with one hundred and ninety-seven pancakes!"

I knew George would fade in the end. He was a strong starter, but not much of a finisher. I pulled my pants up and cinched them with my soggy belt.

"In second place," Sammy bellowed.

This was the one I was really worried about. Franny and Dr. Fuzzwonker were formidable opponents.

"Franny and Dr. Fuzzwonker with two hundred and fifty-one pancakes!"

Wow. Two hundred and fifty-one! I didn't even think that was possible. Floyd and I had never come close to 252 pancakes in ten minutes.

"And in first place for the Fizzies vs. Food competition. . . ," Sammy said. She paused so long I thought she was going to a commercial break.

"The winner with four hundred and twelve pancakes, and the undisputed champions of the known universe . . . Floyd and Harold!"

The crowd went wild. Four hundred and twelve pancakes! It was more pancakes than anyone had ever eaten in ten minutes, a real achievement.

Floyd sat up and rubbed his belly.

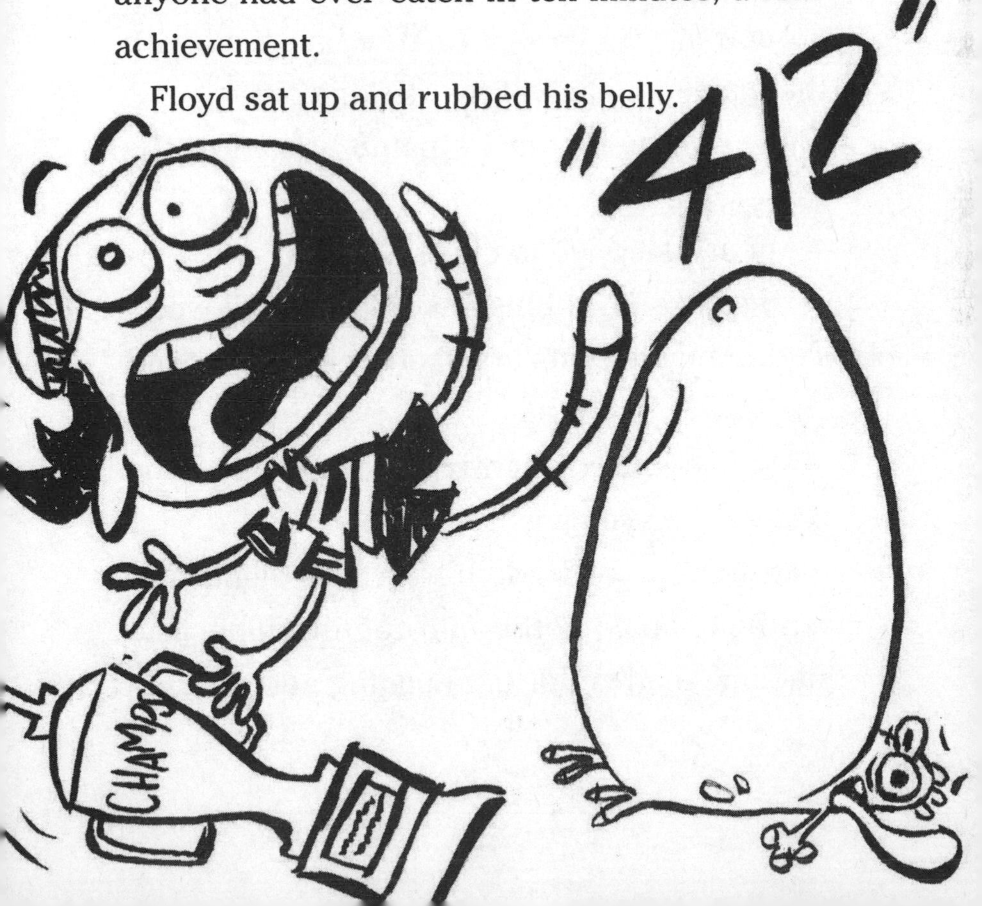
"412"
CHAMPS

"We did it, little buddy!" I said. "We won all the fame! And you get to create your own Fizzy flavor!"

There was a lot of celebrating for our amazing victory, and then everyone gathered around the Fizzomatic machine. The first bottle that would come down the line was going to contain Floyd's brand-new flavor. It would have Floyd's name on the bottle.

Floyd sat up on my shoulder and wobbled around. It was harder to stay balanced with that giant stomach of his sticking out.

"He's come up with a name," I said to the gathered crowd.

My dad stepped in close. "Do tell."

"He'd like to call his flavor Fireball Floyd," I said. "And he wants hot sauce, cinnamon, and gunpowder in there."

My dad looked slightly aghast, but then he nodded. "As you wish."

He went to work adding the ingredients and setting a single bottle into the machine. The machine made a lot of chugging and clicking noises, and then the bottle appeared out the other side with a *ding!*

My dad picked it up and walked it over to us. The old words had been removed and the new ones were printed right there on the bottle: Fireball Floyd.

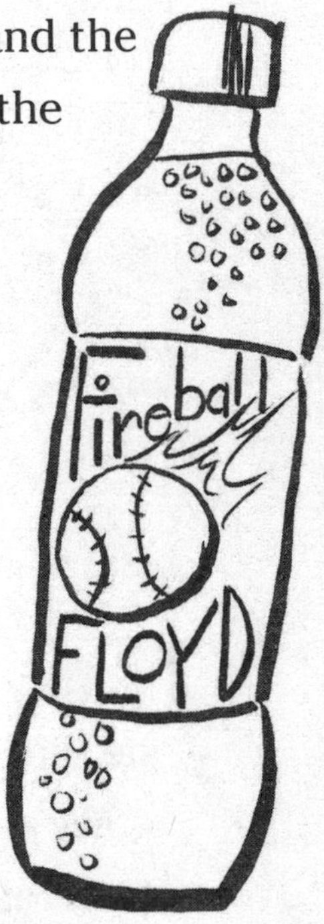
Fireball
FLOYD

"Wow! It's real!" I said. Sammy came over and opened the first bottle as we all watched in anticipation.

"Are you sure you're ready for this?" Sammy asked Floyd. The little guy had to be parched beyond belief. He'd just eaten 412 pancakes.

Floyd took the bottle in his paws. It rested on his round belly.

"Everyone stand back!" my dad said. "There's no telling what a bottle of Fireball Floyd will do."

I hadn't thought of that, and it struck me that Floyd was standing on my shoulder. He might blow my whole ear off if the burp was big enough.

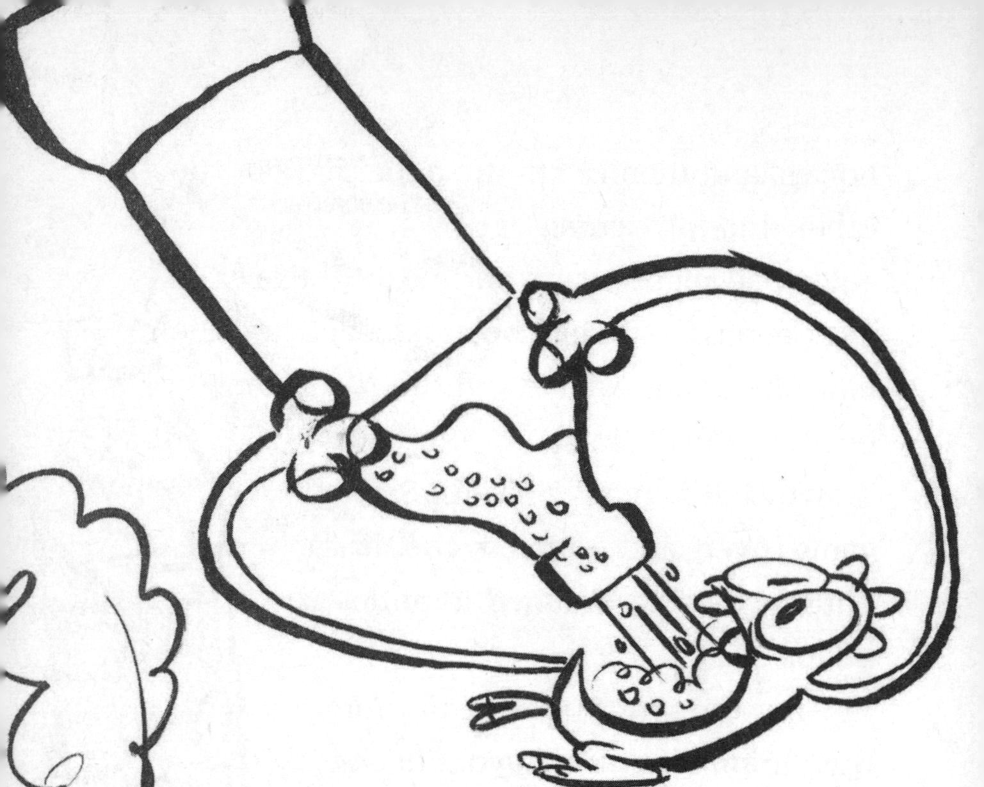

He started chugging in big gulps, and while he did, I set him on the ground to be safe.

Floyd drank the whole bottle down and then dropped it on the ground next to him. His face got red and his stomach made some zingy noises like fireworks were going off in there. He looked up at me and steam poured out of his ears.

"Are you okay,

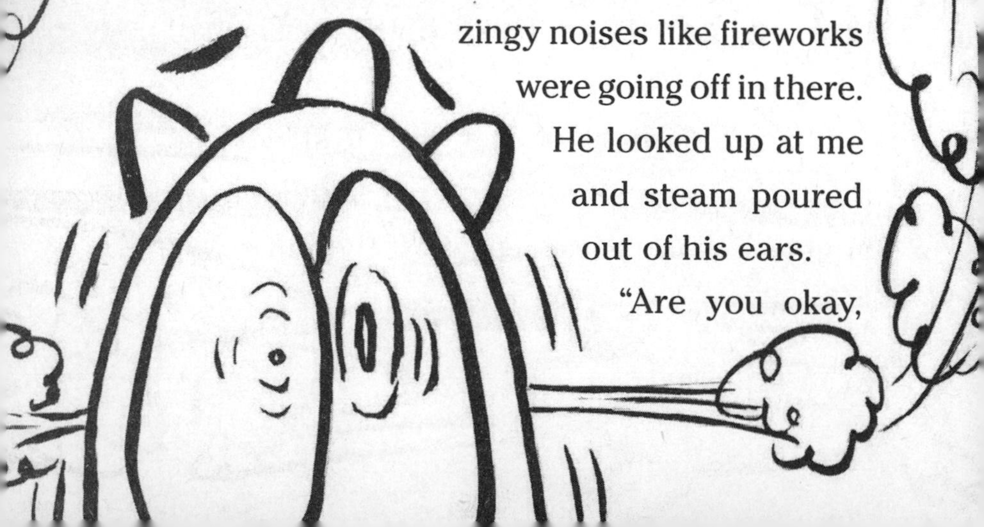

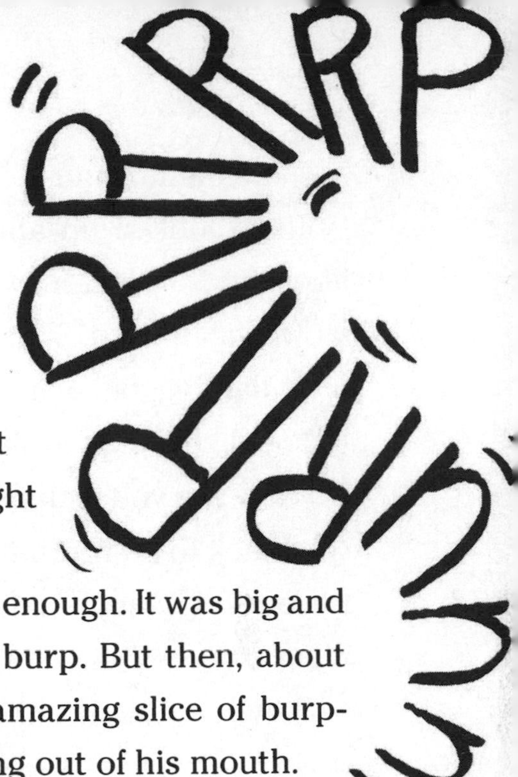

my best good buddy?"

Floyd didn't answer, but he was at least nice enough to turn away from me before he burped. Otherwise it would have landed right in my face.

It started out normal enough. It was big and loud, but it was just a burp. But then, about six seconds into this amazing slice of burpdom, fire started coming out of his mouth.

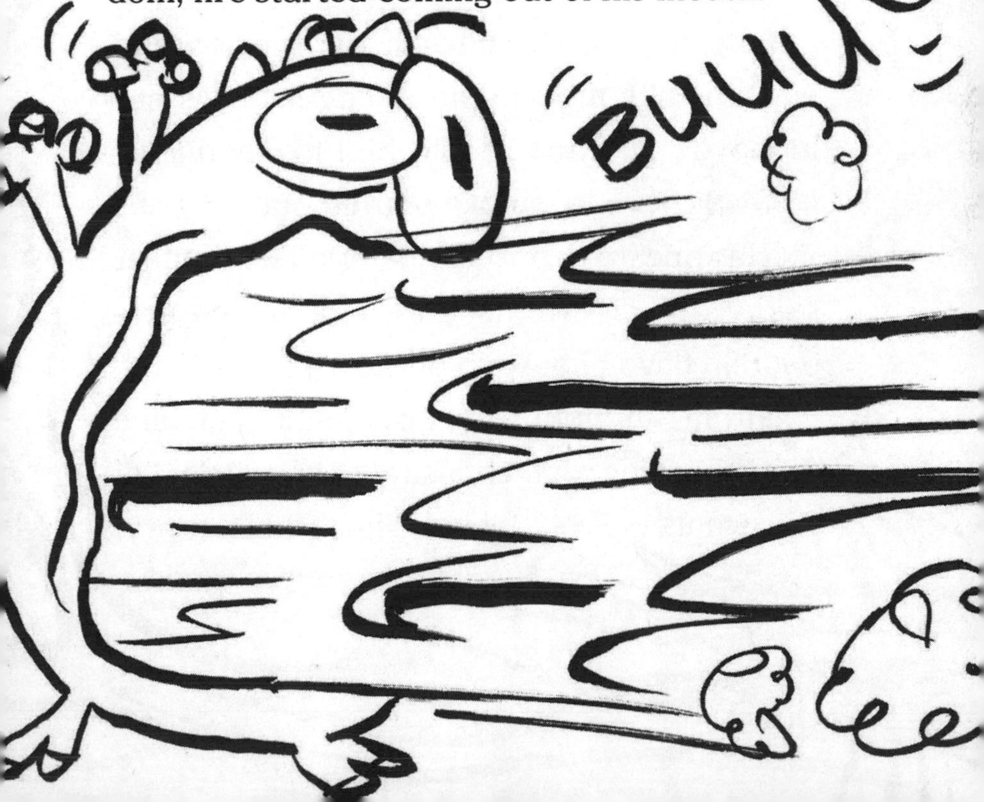

"It's a flaming burp!" Sammy said. "No way!"

Floyd looked up and shot a stream of fire about twenty feet into the Fizzopolis sky. And wow, was it loud. Thirteen seconds later, the first flaming burp in the history of flaming burps died. I leaned down real close.

"How are you feeling?" I asked. His stomach was back to its normal size, so the burp must have used pancakes as fuel and burned them all up.

"Much better, thank you," Floyd said.

Dr. Fuzzwonker walked up to Floyd and put a stethoscope on his chest. Floyd giggled, and when he did, my dad put a tongue depressor in Floyd's mouth and told him to say *ahhhh-hhh*. A little more smoke poured out.

"He appears to be just fine," Dr. Fuzzwonker said. "But this will need to be a limited production flavor. Like one bottle a year."

Within an hour the Fizzomatic machine was churning out thousands of bottles of Fuzzwonker Fizz again. The whole world of Fizzopolis was alive with energy. Every conveyor belt was moving. Every Fizzy was working. And there was more burping than ever. We'd all been waiting for Fuzzwonker Fizz, so we might have overdone it a little on that first night.

Between burps I remembered something I'd completely forgotten.

"Hey, Dad. You said the Snootralizer had a weird side effect. What was it?"

Dr. Fuzzwonker got very quiet and wouldn't answer me. "Oh, it's nothing. It probably won't even work."

THREE DAYS LATER

Sammy and I found our bikes hidden outside the Snood Candy Factory and rode them to the Pfluger Mart, where we found a dozen flavors of Fuzzwonker Fizz back on the shelves. In the parking lot we saw a mob of kids standing around the one and only Garvin Snood. He was telling them all about how Snoodles

had taken over the world and his dad was buying him a Maserati and a speedboat and a hovercraft.

"This is part of the newest batch, fresh off the assembly line," Garvin said. He sneered at me and Sammy, and I heard Floyd growl from inside my backpack. "Go ahead, they're free. It's not like I don't have tons of them."

All the kids standing there just looked at the packages. They seemed to have gotten

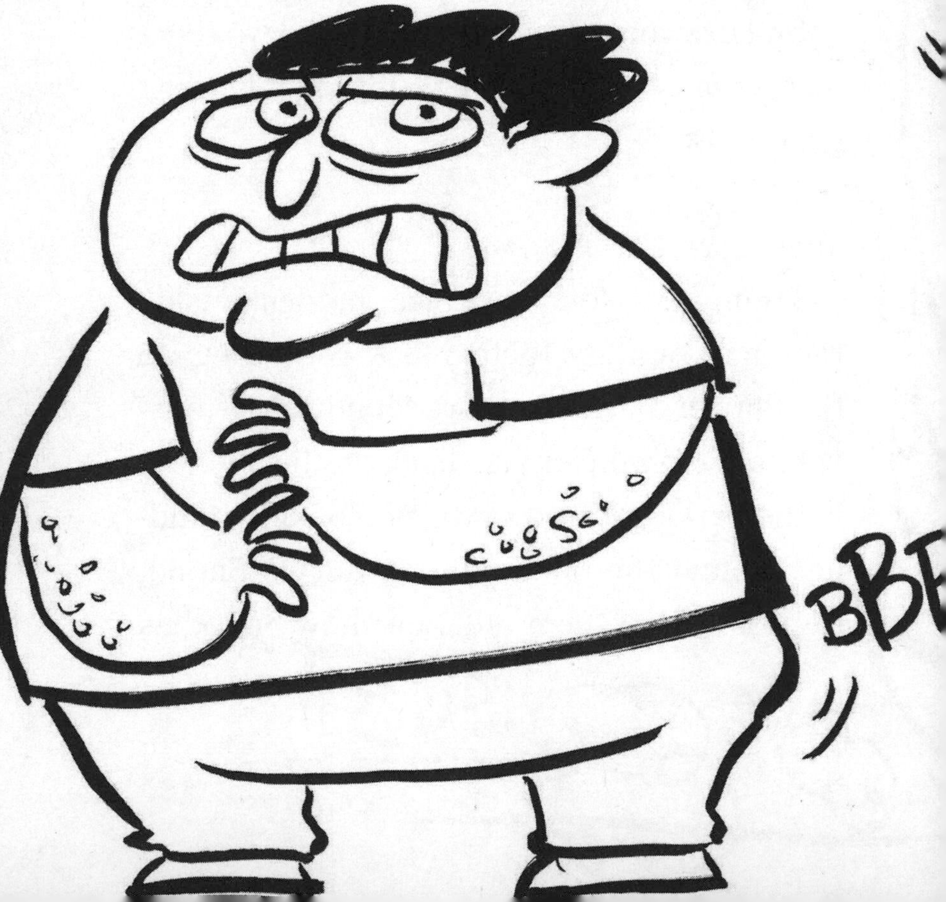

tired of Snoodles, but Garvin tore one open and munched like a maniac.

Then Garvin got a funny look on his face.

Then Garvin farted.

It was loud, and weirdly long. Like twenty seconds long.

He was already riding that giant goofy bike of his back to the Snood Candy Factory before that strange fart came to an end.

So now we know what the Snootralizer did

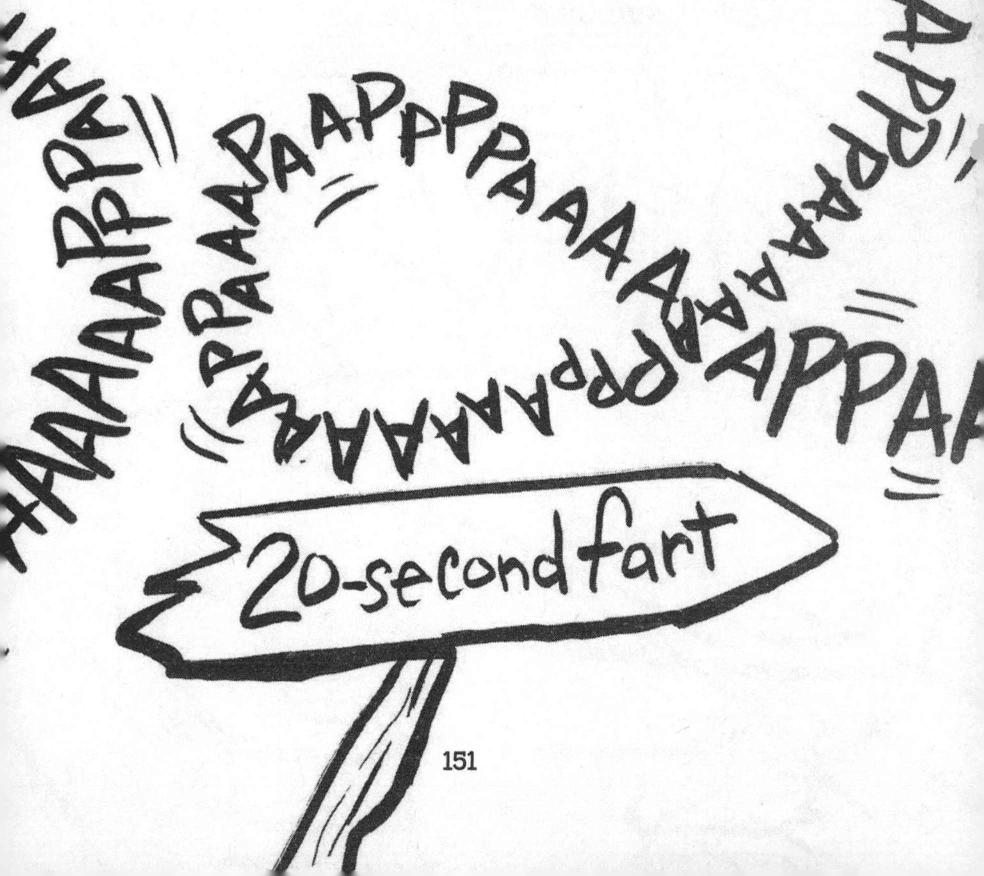
20-second fart

to all those Snoodles. There's not a kid in Pflugerville who will eat one now. It's just too stinkin' weird! And I do mean stinkin'.

"Should we go see Miss Yoobler and have her shoot water at us with the hose?" I asked.

"That's a great idea," Sammy agreed. "And then we'll get a Pfluger burger and go bowling. I love summer!"

We rode off through town, the sun shining, three knuckleheads looking for adventure on a perfect summer day.

The End

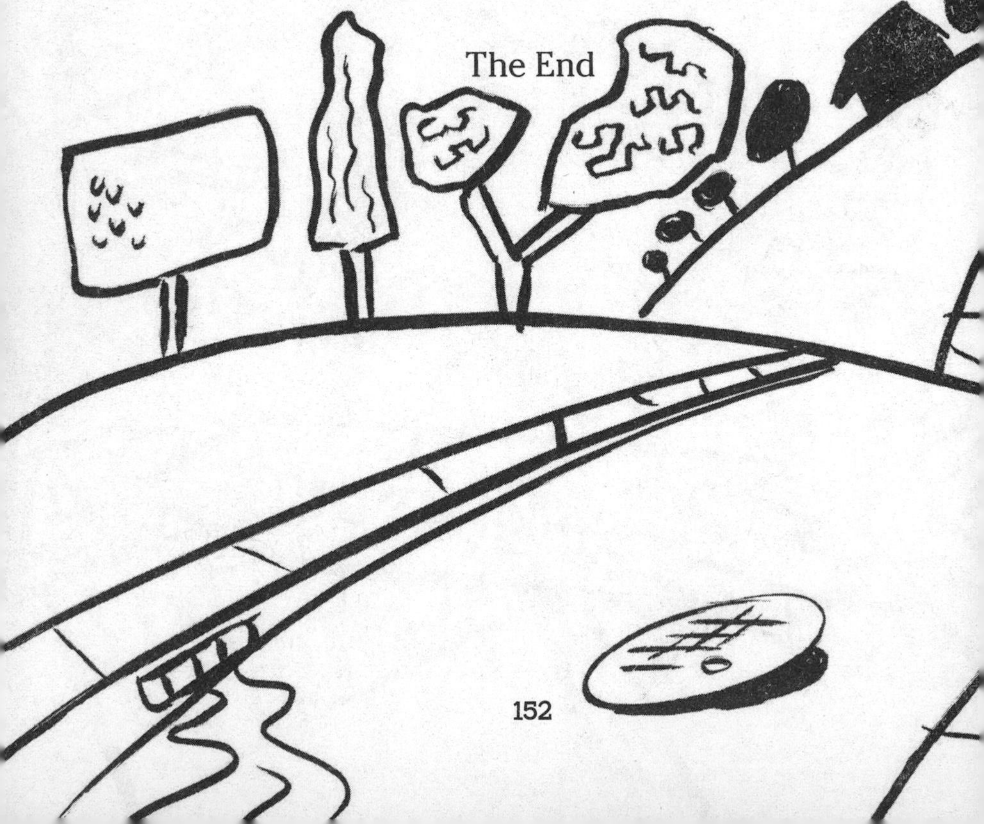

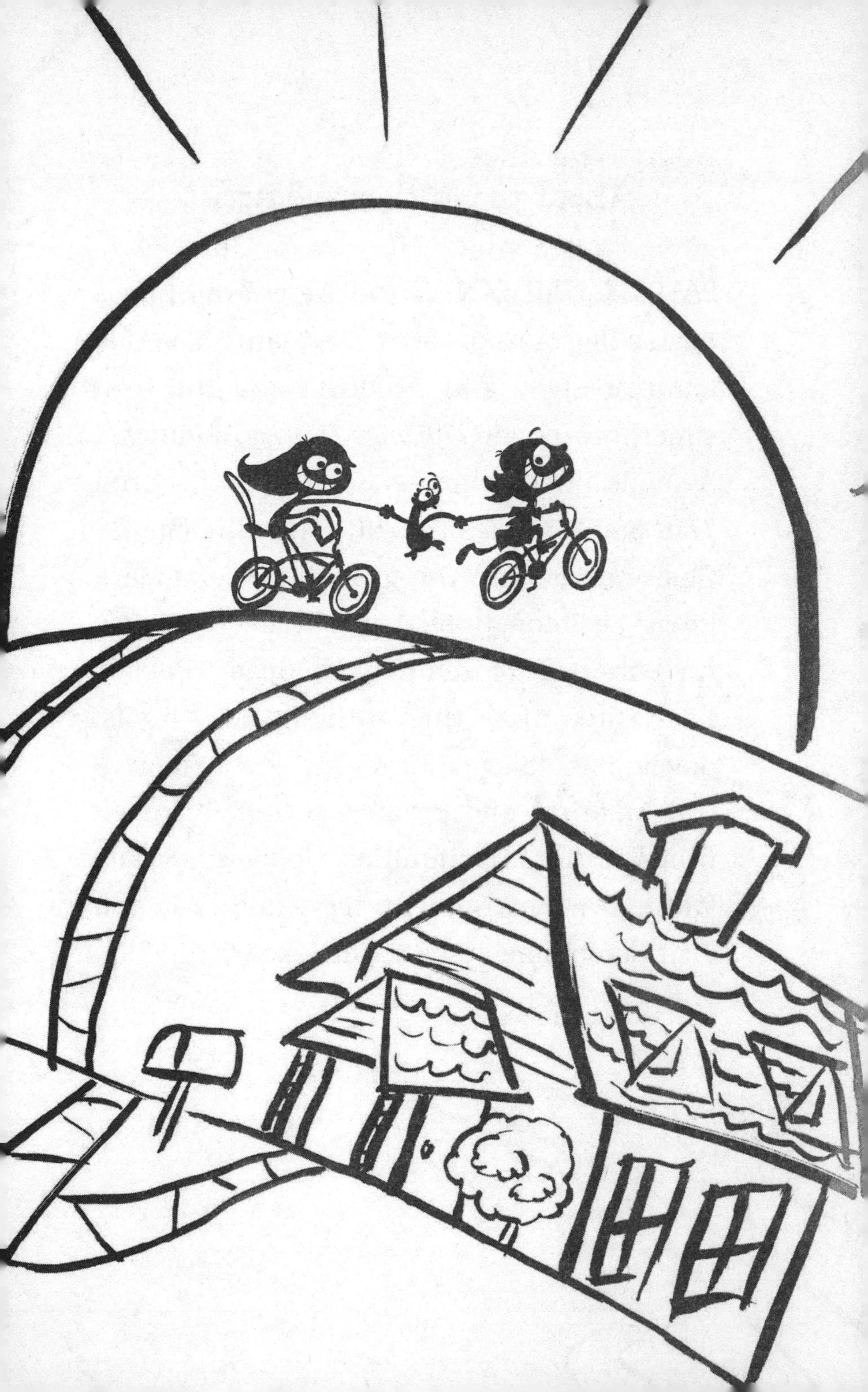

About the Author and Artist

PATRICK CARMAN is the *New York Times* bestselling author of the acclaimed series Land of Elyon and Atherton and the teen superhero novel *Thirteen Days to Midnight*. A multimedia pioneer, Patrick authored *The Black Circle*, the fifth title in the 39 Clues series, and the groundbreaking Dark Eden, Skeleton Creek, and Trackers series. An enthusiastic reading advocate, Patrick has visited more than a thousand schools, developed village library projects in Central America, and created author outreach programs for communities. He lives in Walla Walla, Washington, with his family. You can visit him online at www.patrickcarman.com.

BRIAN SHEESLEY is a five-time Emmy Award–winning director, animator, and designer of some of the most popular animated cartoon shows ever, including *Futurama*; *Camp Lazlo!*; *King of the Hill*; *Fanboy and Chum Chum*; *Regular Show*; and *The Simpsons*. He lives in Los Angeles, California, with his family.

Also available as an ebook.

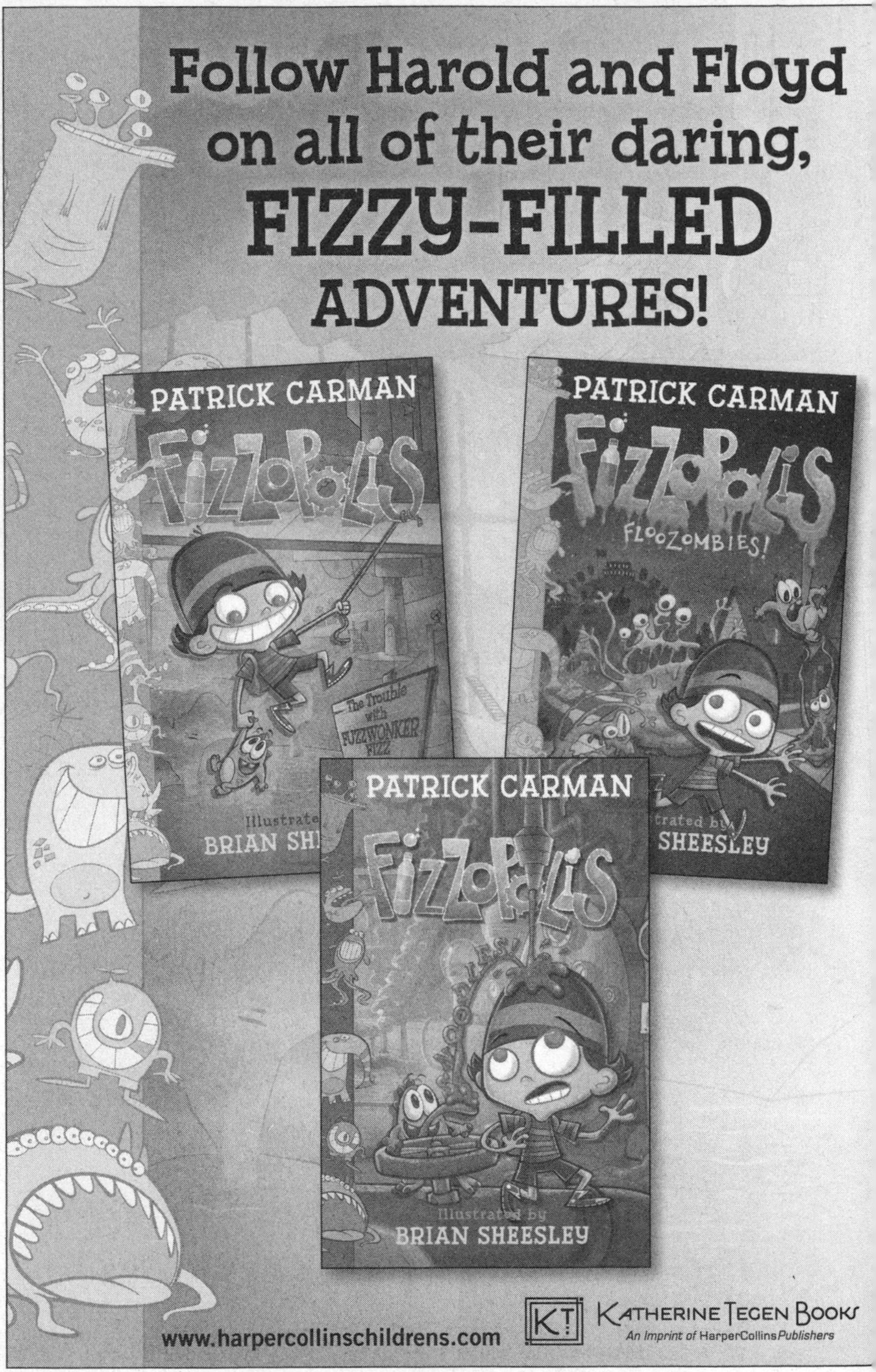
Follow Harold and Floyd on all of their daring, FIZZY-FILLED ADVENTURES!
PATRICK CARMAN
FIZZOPOLIS
The Trouble with FUZZWONKER FIZZ
PATRICK CARMAN
FIZZOPOLIS
FLOOZOMBIES!
SHEESLEY
PATRICK CARMAN
FIZZOPOLIS
Illustrated by
BRIAN SHEESLEY
www.harpercollinschildrens.com
KATHERINE TEGEN BOOKS
An Imprint of HarperCollinsPublishers